# CROWNED
# WITH LOVE

## From the library of

Name_____

Address_____

_____

_____

# THE ROMANTIC NOVELS OF

# BARBARA CARTLAND

## CROWNED WITH LOVE

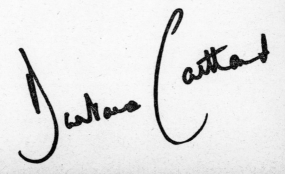

Eaglemoss Publications Limited,
7 Cromwell Road,
London SW7 2HR

First published 1985

© Barbara Cartland 1985

Set in Sabon
Made and printed in Great Britain by
Richard Clay (The Chaucer Press) Ltd,
Bungay, Suffolk

ISBN 0 947837 58 2

# AUTHOR'S NOTE

Macedonian is a South Slavic language, one of the state languages of Yugoslavia, used principally in the People's Republic of Macedonia. In the mid-1960s it was spoken by about 1,000,000 native speakers, including a sizable population in South-western Bulgaria and northern Greece.

Macedonian serves about 300,000 Albanians and Turks who live in Yugoslavia. The language has nothing to do with the Macedonian of classical antiquity, which had long since been replaced by Greek, probably a closely-related language, when the Slavs over-ran the area and settled there permanently in the 7th century.

The records start with the earliest Old Church Slavonic manuscripts (10th–11th centuries), whose language betrays local Macedonian features not generally thought to have been characteristic of the 9th century Thessalonian dialect on which SS Cyril and Methodius presumably based their writings.

From the late 12th century, Macedonians wrote in the standardised types of artificial Slavonic used, with minor variations by all Orthodox South Slavs. While a slightly more popular style appears in a few 17th century translations, no text approximating the spoken language is known before about 1790.

# CROWNED WITH LOVE

Giōna, younger daughter of Her Royal Highness Princess Louise of Greece, is shocked and horrified when
she is ordered by Queen Victoria to be the bride of King
Ferdinand of Slavonia.

She has no choice in the matter because if she refuses the
Queen will insist that her elder sister Chloris, who is secretly
engaged and madly in love, will have to go instead.

Giōna sets off for Slavonia, very suspicious that she is
not being told the truth of why it is so important for her
to be married so quickly, and only when on top of the
Albanian mountains the Royal train which is carrying her
is bombed, does she learn there is a claimant to the throne
who is in fact a Slavonian and who is known as *The
Invisible One*.

How Giōna encounters and saves the life of *The Invisible One*, how she finds when she reaches the capital
that life with King Ferdinand would be completely and
absolutely intolerable, and how *The Invisible One* saves
her, is all told in this thrilling 374th book by Barbara
Cartland.

# CHAPTER ONE
## 1876

Giōna came into the Sitting-Room where her sister was sewing diligently.

"Mama is late!" she said. "I do hope the Queen is not being disagreeable to her."

"Disagreeable?" Chloris enquired. "Why should she be?"

"One never knows with the Queen," Giōna answered, "and Mama is frightened of her – she always has been."

"I always thought Her Majesty was very fond of Mama," Chloris said demurely, "who is, after all, her God-daughter."

Giōna did not bother to argue, but she had one of her strange feelings which the family often laughed about, that her mother's visit to Windsor Castle was not the pleasant, social occasion it was expected to be.

Her Royal Highness Princess Louise of Greece had been brought up to be in awe of the redoubtable and, to most people, extremely formidable Queen Victoria.

It was said that her own son, the Prince of Wales, trembled before he entered her presence, and this was certainly true of most of her less important relatives.

Although it was true she had been kind in her own way to Princess Louise when she and her husband had been obliged to flee from their own country to come to

England and had presented them with a 'Grace and Favour' house, they were none the less in awe of their benefactor.

As Giōna sat down in the window-seat so that she could feel the warmth of the sunshine coming through the open casement she tried to tell herself her fears concerning her mother were unnecessary.

And yet she knew that, as she often did, she was being perceptive, or what was called 'clairvoyant', and that something was wrong.

Very lovely, Giōna took after her father and her features had the perfection of a Greek goddess, while her eyes seemed to have all the mystery that was associated with that unhappy and often divided country.

The beauty of her elder sister, Chloris, was however very different.

She looked English, very English, and resembled her mother, with fair hair, blue eyes and a perfect pink-and-white complexion.

Giōna often said it was ridiculous for her to have a Greek name and she should in fact have been christened 'Rose', or 'Elizabeth', or 'Edith'.

"Papa chose our names," Chloris would explain, "and of course, being Greek, he wished to be patriotic."

"Papa's mother was English," Giōna would reply, "so actually we are only a quarter Greek, however much we may boast about it."

Chloris would not answer because she disliked arguing, and anyway she always came off worst in a duel of words with her younger sister.

Giōna was the clever one of the family and Princess Louise often sighed because they could not afford the Tutors necessary to teach her younger daughter more of the subjects in which she was interested, and yet knew so little.

"Why could I not have been a boy, Mama?" Giōna

asked. "Then I could have gone to a Public School like Eton, and perhaps to Oxford."

Princess Louise should have laughed, but instead she said seriously:

"I wish I could have given your father a son. At the same time, darling, he was very proud of his two beautiful daughters, and always said you resembled his great-grandmother who was acclaimed during her lifetime as being the most beautiful woman in Greece, and the personification of Aphrodite."

"It must have been lovely for her to have so many people to admire her," Giōna answered.

Princess Louise thought with a wry smile that her younger child invariably put her finger on the painful spot in any argument to which there was no reply.

Living so quietly, as they were obliged to do, and having so little money that every penny had to count, they could not entertain and were seldom asked to parties for the simple reason that few people knew of their existence.

There had however been by the greatest good fortune, when Chloris was attending at Windsor Castle the one social function to which she and her mother were invited once a year, a young man who had fallen madly in love with her.

He was a younger son of the Duke of Hull, and from the first moment he looked at Chloris he found it impossible to look away.

They had danced together and the following morning he had called at the small Grace and Favour house.

Chloris had been sitting waiting for him starry-eyed and with fingers that trembled a little because she was so excited.

To the two young people in love the world was so glorious and so thrilling that they had no doubts that they would live happily ever after.

It was only Princess Louise who was apprehensive and worried as to whether the marriage would be allowed.

She had, in fact, been so nervous of approaching the Queen on Chloris's behalf that she made herself ill, and Giōna asked:

"Why cannot the Duke see the Queen instead of you, Mama? I can think of no reason for you to be so upset."

"It is correct for me as a member of the Royal Family to approach the Queen, rather than somebody from outside," the Princess had explained.

Then clasping her hands together, and with a note of agony in her voice she added:

"Giōna, what shall we do if Her Majesty refuses to allow Chloris to marry John? You know it will break her heart!"

"If the Queen does anything so cruel and beastly," Giōna said, "they will simply have to run away together."

Princess Louise looked shocked.

"Of course Chloris could not do anything like that!" she said firmly. "It would cause a terrible scandal, and Her Majesty would be furious!"

Fortunately her fears were groundless.

Queen Victoria had given her permission for Chloris to marry Lord John Cressington, and she was over the moon with happiness.

They would have been married almost immediately if Lord John had not been in mourning for his mother and there could be no question of their announcing their engagement until the customary twelve months had elapsed.

"That means," Princess Louise had said, "you will have to wait until the beginning of April for the announcement, and I should think the actual ceremony could take place some time in the summer."

"I will be married in May!" Chloris said firmly. "How can we go on waiting and waiting, Mama? And John is longing for me to meet all his relatives, which I am unable to do now that the Queen has put this ridiculous ban of silence on us so that we cannot tell everybody as we want to."

Princess Louise did not reply because she understood how frustrating it was.

At the same time, she kept thinking how lucky they had been that the Queen had acquiesced without making the fuss she had feared she would about Royalty marrying a commoner.

The truth was that the reason Her Majesty had not been ruled by her often expressed opinions on the subject was that she did not consider her God-daughter Princess Louise of any real consequence.

Prince Alpheus was only distantly connected by birth with the Royal Family of Greece and now that the King of his country was a Dane, his family was no longer important politically or even socially.

In fact, when soon after reaching England Prince Alpheus died his funeral was so sparsely attended by European royalty that his wife had taken it as an insult.

However she had been so unhappy at losing the husband she loved that she had kept her feelings about the disrespect he had been accorded to herself.

She did not discuss it with her two daughters, but Giōna had sensed what her mother was feeling, and in consequence had been more demonstrative than usual in an effort to alleviate her suffering.

It was impossible for her not to realise how little she and her sister counted when their father had died unmourned and almost unnoticed.

But now Chloris was happy with the thought of her wedding drawing nearer day by day, and because there was so little money the whole household was sewing diligently to provide her with at least an adequate, if not over-generous trousseau.

"I am sure when the time comes for your engagement to be announced, and the Queen realises the imminence of your marriage," Princess Louise said, "she will offer to pay for your wedding-gown. I know it is what she has done for a number of brides in the family. If she does not do so, it will make it very difficult for us to find the money for a really beautiful and expensive gown."

"I know that, Mama," Chloris answered, "but the brides to whom the Queen has been so generous were all marrying Royalty."

There was a moment's silence as Princess Louise and Giōna knew this was the truth.

Practically every throne in Europe was occupied by Queen Victoria's descendants, and she regularly expressed her approval by giving a very handsome gift to the bride-groom and a trousseau to the bride.

"Anyway what does it matter?" Chloris had asked after a little pause. "If the Queen will not give me my gown, it will not prevent me from marrying John, and he thinks I look lovely in anything!"

Perhaps Giōna told herself optimistically, the reason for the Queen sending for her mother now was to tell her that she would help with Chloris's trousseau.

There were only thirty days to wait before the announce-ment of the engagement could appear in 'The London Gazette', and if somebody near to Her Majesty pointed this out, there was no reason why she should not feel kindly towards the daughter of her God-child.

"That must be the explanation, of course it is!" Giōna decided.

Then a little voice inside her, and what she often thought of as her 'third eye', told her that it was some-thing more important than a gown for Chloris.

There was however, no point in saying so aloud and upsetting her sister.

Instead she just sat in the sunshine, looking out onto the small, unimpressive garden in front of the house and wondering why her mother should be away for so long.

Then at last there was the sound of horses' hoofs and wheels, and a moment later Giōna saw the Royal Carriage drawn by two white horses which had been sent from Windsor Castle to collect her mother, draw up outside the front door.

She jumped to her feet saying excitedly as she did so!

"Here is Mama at last! Now we shall know the worst."

She ran from the room without waiting for her sister to reply, and opened the front door before the footman in his cockaded hat had descended from the box to rap sharply, as he intended to do, on the knocker.

His hand was in fact, raised when Giōna appeared at the door.

He smiled as if at her impetuosity and turned back to open the carriage door for Princess Louise.

She stepped out and stopped in her charming, considerate manner to thank both the footman and the coachman who had brought her from the Castle, who both raised their hats in acknowledgement.

Then she walked the short distance to the front door to where her daughter was waiting.

"You are back, Mama!" Giōna cried unnecessarily. "What a long time you have been!"

"I was afraid you might be worried, darling," Princess Louise said kissing her cheek.

She did not say any more, but Giōna looked at her mother apprehensively, and followed her into the Sitting-Room where Chloris was just putting down her sewing before running to kiss her mother.

"Giōna has been fussing about you, Mama," she said,

"but I am sure there is a good reason why you have been longer than we expected."

Princess Louise took off the cape which covered her slim figure and handed it to Giōna to put on a chair.

Then she sat down and awed a little by her silence, even Chloris looked at her with a worried expression.

"What has happened, Mama? You must tell us," Giōna said impatiently. "I felt sure while I was waiting for you that something had gone wrong."

"It is all right – at least I hope it is!" Princess Louise replied.

Giōna's eyes were on her mother's face, and now as the Princess seemed to be feeling for words she moved forward to kneel down at her side.

"What has happened, Mama?" she asked in a low voice.

"I have had a rather difficult time," the Princess faltered, "but I know you girls will understand when I say that Her Majesty was very overwhelming!"

"About what?" Giōna asked abruptly.

Princess Louise gave a deep sigh before she replied. Then she said:

"King Ferdinand of Slavonia has applied to the Queen – of course through his Ambassador – for an English wife to share his throne with him."

The way the Princess spoke made both Chloris and Giōna stare at their mother open-mouthed.

There was a silence that seemed to leave them both paralysed before Chloris said quickly:

"Her Majesty is aware that I am engaged?"

"The engagement has not yet been officially announced, and at first the Queen thought it would be in the best interests of everybody if it was conveniently forgotten."

Chloris gave a cry that seemed to echo round the room.

"Are you saying – Mama – that she is – suggesting I should not – marry John?"

"Her Majesty made it very clear to me," Princess Louise replied, "that it was British policy to keep the small countries in the Balkans independent, and that the Slavonian Ambassador has told her that King Ferdinand will find it very difficult to do so unless he has the support of Great Britain and an English wife to prove it."

Chloris screamed again.

"But I am to – marry John – she agreed I could marry John! I would rather – die than marry – anybody else!"

Her voice rose as she spoke and Princess Louise said quickly:

"It is all right, Chloris! I persuaded Her Majesty in the end that it would be impossible for you to break your word, or for her to withhold the permission for your marriage she has already given, but it was – not easy."

She sighed as if the memory of how difficult it had been was very painful, and Giōna slipped her hand into her mother's and held it tightly.

"She was not unkind to you, Mama?"

"Only rather overbearing and I thought for one moment I had failed to save Chloris."

"But you have – saved me? I can marry – John?" Chloris insisted.

Her mother nodded.

"Oh, thank you, thank you, Mama! But how could the Queen have thought of anything so cruel – so horrible as to try to separate us?"

"You must be aware," Princess Louise replied quietly, "that Her Majesty is concerned only with the political situation in Europe."

"Politics or no politics," Giōna said defiantly, "we are human beings, and the Queen has no right to treat us as if we were just puppets to be manipulated at her command!"

15

Princess Louise who had been looking at her elder daughter now looked down at the younger sitting at her feet.

"I know how you feel, darling," she said, "but you must understand that the privilege of being Royal carries with it the penalty of putting duty before everything else."

Giōna had heard this before and she merely said:

"But you saved Chloris, Mama, and it was very, very clever of you!"

"Very clever!" Chloris echoed wiping away the tears which had run down her cheeks because she was so frightened of what might have happened.

"Yes, you are safe and you can marry John," Princess Louise said, "and the Queen has promised, dearest, to pay for your wedding-gown and part of your trousseau."

Chloris now gave a cry of sheer delight, and running to her mother's side put her arms around her neck and bent down to kiss her.

"You are clever, Mama!" she said. "How could you be so wonderful? I can never thank you enough, and I know John will want to thank you too."

The Princess did not respond as eagerly as her daughters expected and it was Giōna who asked:

"What is wrong, Mama? I can see something is still troubling you."

Princess Louise looked down at Giōna's hand holding hers and said gently:

"As you said, I have saved Chloris, but Her Majesty is still intent on saving the independence of Slavonia."

Again there was a little pregnant silence before the Princess went on:

"Her Majesty pointed out to me that she has at the moment no young relative of the right age to be the wife of King Ferdinand except for Chloris, and of course, you, Giōna!"

16

Chloris made an audible gasp as her mother spoke, but Giōna was suddenly very still, her fingers stiff against her mother's palm.

"Did you say .. me, Mama?"

"Yes, dearest. I think you are too young, as I pointed out to Her Majesty, but as she had conceded, as you might say, that Chloris should not marry King Ferdinand, there was nothing I could do but agree that you should do so."

"I cannot believe it!" Giōna gasped.

She rose from her knees as she spoke and walked to the open window as if she was in need of air.

As she stood silhouetted against the sunlight the Princess thought how slim and immature she looked, and yet it had been impossible to withstand the pressure that had been brought to bear by the Queen to agree to the match.

"Giōna is much too young, Ma'am," she had objected, "and although I appreciate how great an honour it is that Your Majesty should even suggest such a match for her, it is really impossible."

"What do you mean – impossible?" the Queen had asked sharply.

The Princess had chosen her words slowly as if she realised that every one was of great importance.

"Giōna will not be eighteen until next month, Ma'am. She has lived a very quiet life and as yet, as Your Majesty is well aware, has taken no part in social affairs."

Princess Louise had paused for a moment knowing that the Queen was listening. But the hostile expression on her face had told her she was not in the least sympathetic.

"I was, in fact," she went on quickly, "about to ask you, Ma'am, if you would permit her to attend a first or second Drawing-Room, and I was hoping that in this way she might be invited to a few of the Balls that will be given for other débutantes this Season."

There was a pause before the Queen replied:

"I would prefer to have sent Chloris to Slavonia, but if, as you have persuaded me, it is impossible for her to break the promise she has given to Lord John Cressington, then Giōna must take her place."

"But, Your Majesty, she is too young!" Princess Louise said again.

"It is not a question of youth or age, my dear Louise," the Queen had replied, "but what is best for Slavonia."

She paused impressively before she answered:

"The choice lies between a young Queen or submission to the overwhelming might of Austrian–German ambition which would add Slavonia to their long and ever-increasing list of dependencies."

As the Queen spoke Princess Louise had known she was defeated, and now she said aloud to the two girls watching her:

"There was nothing I could do, nothing, except agree."

"But Mama, how can I go to live in Slavonia when it is so far away from you, and be married to a man I have never seen?"

"You may like him when you do meet him," Chloris said encouragingly. "After all, he will be coming to meet us all, and you might fall in love with him. It is not as though you were in love with anybody else."

Giōna knew that Chloris was speaking so optimistically because she was so relieved and happy at not having to marry the King herself.

Princess Louise lay back in her chair as if she was suddenly very tired before she said:

"I am afraid there is no question of the King coming here or of our meeting him at all before the wedding."

Giōna turned round from the window.

"What are you saying, Mama?"

"Her Majesty has been convinced by the Ambassador of Slavonia that the situation is urgent and must be coped with immediately. She has therefore decided that you should go out to Slavonia as soon as we can collect together your trousseau, and you will have a State Marriage in their Cathedral so as to make it very clear to the people that the King has the support of Great Britain and of course of Queen Victoria herself."

Giōna did not speak, but her eyes were so wide they seemed almost to fill her face.

The Princess looked at her and said softly:

"I know this is a shock, dearest, but I swear to you I had to agree to what Her Majesty wanted, and I can only pray from the bottom of my heart that you will be happy."

"How could it ever be possible for me to be happy in such circumstances?" Giōna asked.

"You must try," the Princess said firmly.

"Why should we obey the Queen? Why should she order our lives about as if we had no human feelings and were just made of wood or stone?" Giōna asked angrily.

She knew as she spoke that it was all very wrong and that what the Queen had proposed to her mother was inhuman, a nightmare from which she was finding it impossible to awake.

Quite suddenly she stamped her foot.

"I will not do it, Mama! I will run away and you can tell the Queen that you cannot find me."

The words seemed to ring out round the room. Then after a long pause Princess Louise said very quietly:

"In that case, Giōna, I am quite certain Her Majesty will insist on Chloris going to Slavonia, as was her original intention."

.  .  .  .  .  .  .

Having spent a sleepless night, Giōna, pale-faced and with dark lines under her eyes, came down to breakfast.

There was only Chloris in the small room leading off the kitchen where they had their meals and the Princess had obviously finished and left.

Yesterday evening, after their mother had said that, if she would not marry the King, Chloris would be obliged to do so, Giōna had left the Sitting-Room and run upstairs to her own bedroom.

She had locked herself in and refused to come out, despite pleas both from her mother and her sister.

Now as Chloris's anxious eyes went towards her she felt a little embarrassed and helping herself to bacon and eggs from the heated dish on the sideboard she said as she walked to her place at the table:

"I am sorry, Chloris, but I had no wish to talk to anybody last night."

"Of course, I understand," Chloris said, "and, dearest, I am sorry, desperately sorry for you – but you know I cannot – give up John."

"No, of course not," Giōna replied.

"Perhaps it will not be as bad as you think," Chloris went on hopefully, "and, after all, you will be a Queen!"

Her sister did not reply.

"I used to think we should be buried alive here where we would see nobody but the decrepit old inhabitants of the other houses like our own for the rest of our lives. Then by a miracle I found John for, as he has said so often, he only went to that party because his father was ill and his mother asked him particularly to escort her. Otherwise he would have made every excuse not to be present."

"I know exactly what you are saying," Giōna said in a low voice, "but I think I would rather be an old maid than married to a man who could easily be my father!"

Chloris looked up sharply.

"What are you saying?"

"I thought it would be unlikely that you would know the King's age," Giōna replied, "and Mama very skilfully avoided talking about it, but actually he will be fifty-two next birthday!"

"I do not believe it!" Chloris exclaimed. "Surely he should have a wife by now?"

"He has been married," Giōna answered, "but she died two years ago and that is why they are now able to ask for a Queen who will be of value to the nation."

Chloris did not speak and after a moment Giōna went on:

"And that is what I am to be – a bundle tied up in the Union Jack and handed to him by Queen Victoria like a prize in a Cattle-Show. Like a Farmer's mantelpiece, I shall be plonked down on the throne for all to see!"

Chloris sighed before she said:

"Surely there must be somebody available who is older than you?"

Giōna shook her head.

"No, the Queen was speaking the truth when she told Mama there was no one else. I went downstairs when you were all asleep last night and read Papa's books on the 'Royal Families of Europe' and of course Debrett."

She sighed before she went on:

"I went through them with a fine toothcomb. Every English Princess is either already married or else so decrepit that they would be too old even for King Ferdinand!"

"If he is really as old as that, then he would be too old for me. After all, I am only two years older than you are!" Chloris said.

"Of course," Giōna agreed, "but it does not matter what age one is. It is the Union Jack which counts."

She spoke bitterly and pushed aside her plate as if it was impossible to eat any more.

"At least you will be a Queen," Chloris said again, as

if she was trying to find something consoling she could say.

"I cannot think that is going to be very amusing," Giōna replied. "I remember Papa telling me about Slavonia when we were doing the history of the Balkans and, although it is very beautiful, it did not seem to have much else to recommend it."

She was silent for a moment before she said:

"If it had been Hungary, for instance, there would have been wonderful horses to ride, or if I could live in Greece, I should be perfectly happy, whatever the age of my husband, exploring the wonders of the past and believing I was part of the glories that have never been forgotten."

"The King of Greece is not Greek," Chloris remarked.

"And the King of Slavonia is not Slavonian."

She thought Chloris looked surprised and explained:

"Actually he is an Austrian. He was asked to take over the Kingdom many years ago when apparently there was no one in direct line to inherit the throne."

"How do you know all this so quickly?" Chloris asked.

"I have always been interested in the history of Europe," her sister replied, "and you know Papa adored genealogy and followed the lines of all the Royal Houses right up to the present day. He wrote it all down and he used to read it to me."

She sighed and went on:

"Papa also said it was good for me to know about our neighbours, especially those who were adjacent to Greece. And as he taught me so many different languages, I shall not find it hard to learn Slavonian."

"Do you intend to learn it?" Chloris asked in surprise.

"Of course!" Giōna replied. "I expect they speak German at Court, but I have every intention of being able to converse with the Slavonians over whom I shall rule."

Chloris laughed.

"Over whom King Ferdinand rules! I cannot believe he will let you do much ruling!"

Just for a moment Giōna seemed nonplussed. Then she said:

"All the same, I intend to speak Slavonian so that I can talk to the ordinary people. There are some notes Papa made about their language and apparently it is a mixture of Serbian which I can speak fluently, Albanian which I can understand and, believe it or not, Greek!"

"It sounds terrifying to me!" Chloris said. "But then I was never any good at languages, and have no wish to be for that matter!"

She gave a little laugh.

"Thank goodness the only language in which John is proficient is English!"

She put down the cup of tea she had been holding in her hand and said:

"Darling Giōna, I do not need to tell you how grateful I am to you for agreeing to marry the King. I was not exaggerating when I said that I would rather die than have to give up John! I love him so desperately, and because I know he loves me however poor we shall be, we shall be very happy."

"I know you will be," Giōna answered, "and it was stupid of me to think that perhaps one day I would find somebody like John whom I could love and who would love me."

There was a little silence. Then Chloris said:

"I suppose seeing Mama and Papa so happy with each other, that is what we both hoped we would find too. Oh, Giōna, it is not fair that you should be forced to marry an old man just to please the Queen! If you ask me, she is a big, fat spider sitting in Windsor Castle weaving her web over Europe."

"I have counted that in a short time she will have twenty-four Royal Countries directly under her control,"

Giōna said, "because she has provided them with a reigning Queen or a Ruling Princess."

"I suppose that gives her a lot of satisfaction," Chloris replied, "but it is not fair on you, or anyone like us."

"No, of course not," Giōna agreed, "but you have to realise that we are of no importance beside the fact that the right flag is flying over a Palace and that Austria's ambition has been pushed back a step or two."

"Thank goodness I shall be able to live in England," Chloris said.

Giōna poured herself out another cup of tea before she asked:

"What do you think happens now? Did Mama say anything?"

"Oh, I forgot," Chloris said. "She told me last night that as there is such a rush to get you to Slavonia before the whole place blows up, the Queen is giving you your trousseau, as well as giving me part of mine."

"Well, that is generous of her anyway," Giōna said, "although I doubt if the old King will be at all interested in what I wear."

"You never know," Chloris said. "Some men have an eye for a pretty girl, however old they may be."

Giōna shivered.

"I do not want to think about it."

Chloris looked at her sister rather helplessly as if she had no idea what to say next, and as she did so the door opened and the Princess came into the Dining-Room.

"So there you are, Giōna!" she said. "I had no idea you were downstairs and went to your bedroom."

"What is it, Mama?" Giōna asked.

"I have just received a note delivered by hand to say that the Slavonian Ambassador will be calling on us at twelve o'clock and he will be accompanied by Sir Edward Bowden, the British Ambassador to Slavonia who came here, I understand, to plead with Her Majesty . . ."

24

The Princess paused and her daughter finished:

". . . for a bride for King Ferdinand!"

"Exactly!" the Princess agreed.

"You did not tell Giōna, Mama," Chloris said, "how old the King is. He is fifty-two!"

Princess Louise looked embarrassed.

"I am afraid, dearest," she said to Giōna, "it does seem very old, but I believe he is very active."

Giōna rose from the breakfast-table.

"I think, Mama, I would like to go through Papa's Library and see how much more I can find out about Slavonia. If only he was here, he could tell me all the things I need to know."

"Yes, of course, dearest," the Princess agreed, "and I am sure your father would be very proud of you and would tell you that you were doing the right thing."

"I do not have much choice, Mama, do I?" Giōna asked bitterly. "But on one thing I am quite determined: I will not go blindfold into the country, knowing nothing and having no idea of what is going on."

Princess Louise looked surprised.

"Why should you think that anything is 'going on' as you put it?"

"I am sure we would not have been rushed in this extremely undignified manner unless there were something far more serious than King Ferdinand's wanting a wife, and the Austrians and Germans making noises off-stage."

"I do not know what you are saying!" Princess Louise said in a bewildered tone.

"I am not quite certain myself," Giōna replied, "but I have the feeling in my bones that there is something far more sinister and far more menacing than we have been told, and I am sure the Ambassador, and that goes for the English one too, will do everything he possibly can to prevent my knowing about it."

"I do not understand what you are implying," Princess Louise said helplessly.

For the first time that morning, Giōna smiled.

"If there are secrets," she said, "I intend to ferret them out! My 'third eye' tells me not only that they exist, but that they are something that everybody, including the Queen, is trying to keep hidden."

# CHAPTER TWO

The Slavonian Ambassador who like most of the Court was German, was very precise and very pompous in his congratulations to Giōna.

She had the feeling at the same time that the British Ambassador, Sir Edward Bowden was fundamentally somewhat apologetic, but she realised that he was very much intimidated by his Slavonian opposite number and therefore contributed little to the conversation.

After the Ambassador had told her in a long-winded way how much her marriage would mean to the people of his country, and had offered her the felicitations and good wishes of the King, there was at last a pause when Giōna was expected to answer.

For a moment, because she had listened for so long, she did not understand what was expected. Then she said:

"I cannot understand, Your Excellency, why the King has not himself come to England, both to approach the Queen on behalf of his country, and also, of course, to ask me personally for my hand in marriage."

The Slavonian Ambassador looked so surprised that she might have thrown a bomb at him.

Then as he began to puff and blow and again go into a long and complicated explanation, she was quite certain she was not going to hear the truth.

She realised that her mother was upset by the frankness with which she had spoken, and was nervous of her antagonising the Ambassador so that he would make an unfavourable report of her behaviour to the King.

She was however, more concerned with herself than her mother's feelings, and when at last his guttural voice came to a stop she said:

"Is the situation really so critical in Slavonia, Your Excellency, that everything has to be done so quickly?"

This time, to her surprise, Sir Edward Bowden answered before the Ambassador had time to think up what she was certain would be an evasive answer.

"The position, Your Royal Highness, is difficult," he said, "but His Majesty is quite certain, and so are we, that when the news of your marriage is announced to the populace they will be so overwhelmed with delight that there will be no more trouble."

"Trouble? What exactly is the trouble at the moment?" Giōna persisted.

The British Ambassador glanced rather uncomfortably at the Slavonian standing beside him before he replied:

"There is just a little unrest, as is happening in many Balkan countries."

"Unrest about what?" Giōna enquired.

This time there was a definite pause while she was certain both men were thinking how they could evade the question.

Finally the Ambassador said:

"All these things will be explained to Your Royal Highness when you arrive in Dūric, and I am sure the reception you receive once you are on Slavonian soil will be a very pleasant one."

"I certainly hope so," Giōna said. "But there is one thing I must insist upon before I arrive."

The Slavonian Ambassador looked at her as if he

resented the word 'insist' and wondered what she was about to ask.

Before he could speak however Giōna said:

"You will understand, I am sure, that it is a very reasonable request – it is that somebody should teach me Slavonian. I am quick to learn and wish to start at once with, of course, a teacher who is of Slavonian nationality."

"I hardly think that is necessary, Your Royal Highness," the Slavonian Ambassador replied. "His Majesty and all his Court speak German."

"So I have heard," Giōna said coldly, "but I would wish to understand the language of the country in which I am living, and the majority of the King's subjects must naturally be Slavonian."

There was no answer to this and the Ambassador puffed and huffed and repeated several times that it would be very difficult to find a suitable person before she actually arrived in Slavonia.

Then at last the British Ambassador said:

"The new *Aide-de-Camp* to His Majesty who accompanied us to England is in fact, Slavonian."

"If you are referring to Captain Otho Darius, he is far too young. And since he has only just joined us, I am not certain that he would be suitable to instruct Her Royal Highness."

"Everybody else is German," Sir Edward Bowden said quietly, "so unless I am mistaken, I doubt if any of them are at all fluent in Slavonian."

With a bad grace the Slavonian Ambassador gave in.

"Very well," he said, "you can see Captain Darius, and of course he can be dispensed with as soon as we arrive in Dūric."

The way he spoke made Giōna feel that she had won a major victory, and only when the Ambassador had left, again expressing himself effusively on how satisfactory it was for everyone that she was to be the Queen of Slavonia, did Princess Louise ask:

"Why do you make such a fuss, dearest, about learning Slavonian?"

Giōna looked at her mother in surprise.

"But surely, Mama," she said, "you realise it is something Papa would have done. He always felt it mortifying and infuriating to visit any country where he could not speak the language fluently, and he would definitely have been shocked if I had accepted to be the Queen of Slavonia without being able to communicate with any of my husband's subjects."

The Princess had no answer to this, but before Captain Darius arrived the next morning to give Giōna her first lesson she said to her daughter:

"Now listen, Giōna, I think it would be a mistake for you to discuss politics when you are with Captain Darius."

"Why, Mama?" Giōna asked in surprise.

The Princess hesitated and Giōna said:

"What is so secret about the politics of Slavonia? I realised yesterday that the Ambassador was keeping something from me."

"I do not think it is a question of being secret, dearest," the Princess replied. "The British Ambassador explained to me that there was unrest and trouble in the country because a number of people resent being ruled over by what they think of as a foreign King."

"I can understand that."

The Princess looked at her daughter sharply.

"You may understand," she said, "but it would be a great mistake for you to sympathise with them, or in any way fail to support your husband loyally."

"Of course, Mama," Giōna agreed. "At the same time, I cannot understand why so many of the Balkan countries chose Kings from outside their own boundaries. I remember Papa saying years ago that it was a great mistake."

"I think your father was talking about Greece," the Princess replied. "There is no reason to think that King Ferdinand is not an excellent Monarch in every way, and naturally no encouragement must be given to any sort of revolutionaries."

Giōna did not reply and after a moment the Princess went on:

"What is more, dearest, you must be very careful what you say, and if Captain Darius tries to enlist your sympathy because he is a Slavonian, I hope you will make it very clear that you are heart and soul on the side of the King."

"I can hardly be sure of that until I arrive in Slavonia, and see what the King is like, Mama!"

Princess Louise gave a little cry of protest.

"Please, Giōna," she said, "you must not be too independent. You must remember that from now on anything you say and almost anything you think, will be of importance and could be used either for or against you, and of course your husband the King."

Giōna laughed.

"I am sure, Mama, you are exaggerating my importance. After all, the only thing that matters is that I am English and am being sent there by the Queen to hold an umbrella over his head in case he is pushed into becoming part of the Austrian Empire!"

"Giōna, you must not say such things!" the Princess protested.

But Giōna knew that she was really very worried in case she should start off her marriage of convenience on the wrong foot.

What she had not expected was that when Captain Darius arrived she found he was young and an extremely good-looking man of about twenty-five.

31

Having met the Slavonian Ambassador, who was over fifty, she had expected his whole *entourage* to be old, and doubtless as pompous and long-winded as he was.

Instead, when she was told Captain Darius had arrived, and she went downstairs to where he had been shown into the small Sitting-Room, she found herself thinking that he was the first pleasant factor concerned with her wedding she had experienced.

Captain Darius spoke in English with a pronounced accent, but he had an engaging smile, and she thought there was an undoubted look of admiration in his eyes when he saw her.

"I have the honour, Your Royal Highness," he said, "to be appointed by His Excellency to teach you a little Slavonian before you arrive in my country."

He paused before he added:

"And may I say with all respect that we in Slavonia shall be very fortunate to have such a beautiful Queen."

Giōna smiled.

"Thank you," she said, "but I do not want to know only a little Slavonian by the time I arrive in your country, but to speak it fluently."

"I am afraid that might be impossible, as it is a somewhat complicated language," Captain Darius said, "but I will certainly do my best, Your Royal Highness, although I have always before been a pupil, not a teacher."

"I cannot think that Slavonian can be any more difficult than Greek," Giōna said, "and I can speak Serbian, a little Albanian and a certain amount of Macedonian."

Captain Darius seemed to think this incredible, and when they sat down at the table Giōna found to her delight that Slavonian was, as she had said to Chloris, comparatively easy because it was a mixture of all the other languages she knew.

"You are incredible, absolutely incredible, Your Royal

Highness!" Captain Darius said at the end of an hour. "I would like to thank you with all my heart for wishing to know Slavonian, even though I feel you will very seldom use it."

"Why do you say that?" Giōna asked quickly.

For a moment he looked embarrassed as if he had spoken without thinking. Then he said:

"I am sure you are already aware that His Majesty speaks German at Court."

"Yes, I had heard that," Giōna said.

"As the majority of the Courtiers and practically everybody of any importance in the Government is either German or Austrian, the Slavonians seldom hear their own language, except in the streets."

"Is that really true?" Giōna asked.

"Perhaps I should not tell you what you will soon find out for yourself," Captain Darius said.

Giōna lowered her voice.

"I want you to tell me the truth. If we are to work together it will be impossible if each of us is saying one thing and thinking another. Please, Captain, be frank with me."

The Captain gave a sigh.

"It is what I would like to do, Your Royal Highness, but if I am it will, if it becomes known, get me into a great deal of trouble."

"Let me assure you that anything you say to me in confidence will not be repeated," Giōna said. "But I do want to know, and I think that only you can tell me, exactly what is the position in Slavonia, and why this marriage has been arranged with such unseemly haste."

To her surprise, Captain Darius rose to his feet and started to gather his books and papers together.

"I regret, Your Royal Highness, that the hour allotted to us for your lesson has come to an end," he said in a cold voice. "I can only congratulate you on your quick intelligence and the manner in which you have assimilated so many different elements of our somewhat complex language in so short a time."

The way he spoke was so different from his former easy manner that Giōna could only stare at him in astonishment.

Then before she could ask why he had suddenly changed his tone, the door of the Sitting-Room opened and unannounced the Slavonian Ambassador entered.

"Good-morning, Your Royal Highness," she said to Giōna. "Forgive me for my impertinence in walking in without being announced, but although I rang the bell several times, there was no reply."

The way he spoke made Giōna sure that he was lying and she was quite certain he had deliberately not knocked, but had opened the door without doing so and entered the house silently so that he could listen to what was going on.

She had already learnt that Captain Darius's ears were sharper than hers, and she knew from the expression on his face that he had been aware that somebody was listening.

To the Slavonian Ambassador she said:

"You have come at exactly the right time, Your Excellency, because Captain Darius and I have finished, and I found my lesson very interesting except of course there is always a difficulty with verbs and vowels when one starts a new language."

The Ambassador laughed.

"That is indeed true, Your Highness, but I am glad that Captain Darius has proved a good instructor. Do you really wish to carry on?"

"Of course I do!" Giōna replied. "I shall look forward to having my lesson tomorrow morning. I am only sorry that this afternoon I have to go shopping with Mama."

"For your trousseau," the Ambassador said genially. "And that is very important if you are to look beautiful for your new husband."

"Yes, of course," Giōna said. "That is why Mama is taking so much trouble in choosing my gowns."

She made it sound like girlish enthusiasm, but when she looked from the Ambassador to Captain Darius's face, she knew, because his expression was dark and foreboding, that he was appalled, if that was the right word, that she should be the bride of the King.

. . . . . . .

It was not until that evening that Giōna learnt her Mother was not coming with her to Slavonia.

"Not coming to my wedding, Mama?" she exclaimed. "But, why? How could I possibly go without you?"

"I talked the matter over with the British Ambassador," Princess Louise answered, "and while actually Her Majesty had told me she thought it was unnecessary for me to make such a long journey, I had every intention of insisting on accompanying you until Sir Edward persuaded me it would be a mistake."

"Why should he do that?" Giōna asked angrily.

"As you know, Slavonia lies South of Albania and of Serbia, surrounded on other sides by Macedonia. There is, His Excellency said, quite a lot of trouble on the frontiers of the country and while they intend to send a large escort to take you safely to the Capital it would be a nuisance and would create difficulties if the same escort had to take me back after the ceremony was over."

She saw that her daughter was unconvinced and went on:

"Besides, the Ambassador also said that while Her Majesty is sending you in a battleship, which is a great concession on her part, out to Slavonia, she has no wish for the ship to have to wait to bring me back to England."

"Well, I think it is disgraceful, Mama!" Giōna exclaimed. "I do not want to go without you."

"I know, dearest, but you will be well looked after. Sir Edward's wife, Lady Bowden, will chaperon you and the Slavonian Ambassador will of course, travel with you."

"It is wrong .. I know it is wrong for me to go off alone!" Giōna said unhappily. "I had assumed that you would be with me, Mama."

"There is nothing I want more, dearest," the Princess said, "I tried, but there was nothing more I could do to persuade them that you are too young to travel without me."

She sounded so distressed that Giōna said little more to her mother. But to Chloris she raged:

"The whole thing is disgraceful! The Queen has no right to push me out of England in a battleship to all intents and purposes alone, and leave me to fend for myself without anyone to support me in a completely strange country."

"I am sorry, dearest," Chloris said, "I know I should be miserable if I were in your shoes. But Sir Edward and Lady Bowden are English, and I am sure they will look after you."

"I am sure they will!" Giōna said crossly. "Because it suits them to toady to the King!"

She did not say any more, but when she was alone in bed she found herself wondering who she would turn to in Slavonia if she was desperately unhappy.

It was frightening to think that everybody she knew and loved would be hundreds of miles away.

She would be of no personal consequence to anyone, except for the fact that she was British and, as she had said to Chloris, 'tied up in the Union Jack'.

. . . . . . . .

As the days went by far too quickly for comfort, Giōna found herself almost resenting the pretty gowns her

36

mother was buying at the Queen's expense and the exquisite lace-trimmed underclothes which were different from anything she had ever worn before.

What did it matter what she looked like, when she was being married to a man whose only interest in her was that she would 'prop up' what she was convinced now was a rather rocky throne, and with whom she was quite certain she would have nothing in common?

The more she talked with Captain Darius, the more she was convinced that the true picture of the political situation in Slavonia was being kept from her.

What was more, after the first day when the Slavonian Ambassador had crept up on them so unexpectedly, Giōna knew that Captain Darius was too frightened to tell her the truth about anything.

Sometimes he would seem as if he was going to be frank and explain the situation which she was certain existed, but was impossible for her to assess.

Then as if his duty or, perhaps, his fear made him change his mind at the last moment, he would remain silent.

She was certain that he was afraid of being overheard and, often, when she asked some pertinent question about his country, he would glance at the door almost as if he thought there was somebody outside.

One day at the end of the first week while she was having her lesson, she found that what Captain Darius suspected was only too true.

A slight sound in the small hall outside the Sitting-Room made her get up quickly and without warning open the door.

Standing in the hall was another of the Embassy *entourage* who explained quickly and in an obviously embarrassed manner that he had only just arrived with a message for her mother and seeing that the door was open had walked in without ringing the bell.

It was true that sometimes when the weather was fine the door was left open to let in the sunshine, but Giōna was quite certain that when she had gone into the Sitting-Room for her lesson the door was closed.

It was therefore obvious that the intruder had let himself in.

She had taken the message, which was a note to her mother asking her and both Giōna and Chloris to dinner at the Slavonian Embassy, then waited for the bearer of it to leave.

He however looked past her at Captain Darius who was standing in the doorway of the Sitting-Room, and there was an expression on his face which told Giōna without words that he was extremely hostile to the young Slavonian.

In German he said:

"If you have finished your lessons, Darius, I thought you might come back with me to the Embassy."

"Of course," Captain Darius replied. "Her Highness and I have nearly completed our studies for this morning. Perhaps you would wait while I give her a passage to translate before tomorrow."

The other man nodded his agreement, bowed to Giōna, and walked out through the front door to where she could see the carriage which had brought him waiting some distance away.

It was quite obvious that if he had driven up to the door in the ordinary way, they would have heard the horses' hoofs and the sound of the wheels.

But then he would not have been able to enter the house so surreptitiously.

Giōna shut the front door behind him and went back into the Sitting-Room, and as she and Captain Darius tidied the books on the table she asked:

"Why is he spying on you?"

"Because he does not trust me."

"Why should he not trust you?"

"Because I am Slavonian."

Giōna was not surprised at the answer, for it was only what she had expected, and after a moment she asked:

"If they do not trust you, why were you included in the party which came to England to see the Queen? I realise all the others are Austrian or German."

"It was on the insistence of several of the Members of Parliament. They said that at least one member of the deputation should be a true Slavonian. After a great deal of argument and opposition, I was chosen because I was considered too young and inexperienced to be of any danger."

"Danger?" Giōna questioned.

"Not so much physically as politically."

"Why? What is going on? Please tell me."

"I dare not," he said. "Quite frankly, Your Royal Highness, it is more than my life is worth. But because I admire you, may I say that I will do everything in my power to help you, should the need arise, and you can always count on me – although that is not saying very much."

"To me it means a great deal!" Giōna replied. "I am frightened, very frightened of being alone in a strange country with no one to whom I can speak freely and frankly."

"I should be very proud and honoured if you will do that," Captain Darius said. "But if they realised we had had such a conversation as this, I should be instantly removed from my present post and it would be impossible for us ever to meet like this again."

Giōna drew in her breath.

"I understand," she said, "and we must be very, very careful, which is something that has never been necessary before in this house. When you come here next for our lessons, I will lock the door."

The Captain's smile seemed to illuminate his whole face.

"There speaks the practical Englishwoman!" he said. "I never thought of anything so simple as to ask you if we could lock the door!"

Giōna laughed too. Then she said:

"It sounds funny, but it is not really a laughing matter, is it?"

The Captain shook his head.

"No, but there is nothing I can do about it except to offer you my protection if it becomes necessary and to be careful meantime not to be sent away."

"That is really important," Giōna agreed. "If I lose you, then I shall have no one!"

Captain Darius looked at her, and there was an expression in his eyes which made her more apprehensive than she was already.

He was afraid for her, afraid of what lay ahead in the future, and although she longed to beg him to tell her what it was, she knew instinctively that it was something she must not do at the moment.

She had heard enough in her life about political intrigue in the Balkans to realise that there would be no scruples about eliminating anybody who constituted a danger of any sort.

She knew it would be a mistake to underestimate what were the obvious suspicions of the Germans who served the King and who would do everything, however ghastly, to prevent her from trying to withdraw from the marriage which was, in their consideration, vital to uphold the throne.

It was difficult to put it clearly into words, but every night Giōna would lie awake puzzling over what she sensed, but could not substantiate, and she was desperately afraid of what lay ahead of her once she had left England.

40

In the meantime, wedding presents were pouring in to their small house from all sorts of people who had never paid her the slightest attention before.

There were not only those who had been acquainted with her father, but there were gifts from other Embassies, and from a number of her relatives who had never troubled themselves with the impoverished Princess Louise and her two daughters.

"I doubt if you will get a better collection, Chloris," Giōna said to her sister.

"I should be astonished if I get half what you are receiving," Chloris replied. "But after all, everyone wants to know a Queen! In fact, they will all be expecting invitations to stay with you in your grand Palace!"

"I shall welcome them with open arms," Giōna said, "but I have a feeling their wedding presents are designed more to impress Queen Victoria than me. I expect she will want to hear who has been generous enough to ante-up so we had better make a list."

This was certainly prophetic, for a few days later a note came from Windsor Castle to say that the Queen would like to know what presents Giōna had received and to bring with her to luncheon at the Castle any outstanding gift which would be likely to interest Her Majesty.

"The Queen is showing more interest in your marriage than I expected, dearest!" Princess Louise exclaimed.

"I think she has a feeling that I am a valuable weapon of defence between the throne of Slavonia as it is now, and a revolution."

Giōna was not certain exactly what she was saying. She was trying it out on her mother to see how much she knew, and was not surprised when Princess Louise went very pale and said:

"Why should you say such things? Who has been talking to you about a revolution in Slavonia?"

Her reply made Giōna realise that if she was taken seriously it might rebound on Captain Darius.

"I was only joking, Mama," she said quickly. "You know how frequent revolutions are in the Balkans, and it would be quite unnatural if Slavonia never had one."

She had the feeling that her mother gave a little sigh of relief before she said:

"I think it is unlucky to joke in such a way. Revolutions are very frightening things, as your father would tell you if he were alive, and I want you to reign over a peaceful country without there being any fear of your husband being deposed."

"I am sure that is what I can look forward to," Giōna said lightly.

She told herself she must be more careful in future.

It was infuriating however to guess that her mother knew more than she would tell her, and so did Captain Darius, while she was to be kept in ignorance, at any rate until the ring was on her finger and the crown on her head.

Queen Victoria gave her a long lecture on behaving with dignity once she became a Queen, and how she should defer in all things to her husband's wishes.

"You may find your husband because he is Austrian, somewhat dictatorial, especially because he was brought up in Germany," she said.

"Brought up in Germany, Ma'am?" Giōna interrupted. "Nobody told me that before."

"Well, he was, and he served as a soldier in the German Army before he had the opportunity of becoming King of Slavonia."

"Please tell me more about him, Ma'am," Giōna pleaded.

"He has made a very good job of it," the Queen said firmly. "His family was poor and he was the youngest son of his father who was a Grand Duke. It was therefore

42

a great opportunity for him to be made a Monarch in his own right."

"I can see that," Giōna agreed.

"You must support him, dear child," the Queen went on. "You must help him in every way you can and remember, the Germans do not like to be argued with or challenged by their womenfolk."

The Queen gave Giōna a sharp look as if she fancied she was inclined to be aggressive and said:

"You must learn to be quiet, discreet and at times humble. It may not be easy, but I am quite sure that is what King Ferdinand will expect from his wife."

The Queen was unaware that Giōna had stiffened a little as if she resented the idea of being so subservient.

Then because she had no wish for the Queen or anyone else to think she was intensely curious about what was happening in Slavonia, she said:

"I will try to do as you tell me, Ma'am. I know how happy you were in your marriage with Prince Albert."

The Queen's eyes softened.

"I was very, very fortunate to be married to anyone so wonderful, so perfect in every way, and I hope you will be as happy with King Ferdinand."

"That is what I hope too," Giōna said, "and thank you, Ma'am, for your advice."

She curtsied, kissed the Queen's hand, then her cheek.

Only when she had left the Palace did she say to her mother:

"I cannot think why the Germans should despise women to the point where they expect them to be nothing but door-mats!"

Princess Louise looked startled.

"I am sure Her Majesty did not mean you to think that."

"What else am I expected to think?" Giōna asked. "I cannot imagine what it would be like never to have a

43

thought of my own, but have to agree with everything some old man has said as if it were holy writ, straight out of the Bible!"

The Princess gave a little cry.

"Giōna, you are not to talk like that! It is very wrong! I am sure you will find that you and King Ferdinand have a great deal in common that you can talk about and discuss, and he will listen to your opinions as you will listen to his."

"Yes, of course, Mama," Giōna agreed.

The Princess was not aware as she spoke very softly that Giōna was being sarcastic.

When however Giōna went to her bedroom that night she looked at her face in the mirror.

She looked very young with the soft curves of her cheeks and her eyes very large and questioning.

Then as she looked at herself she asked, the words bursting from between her lips:

"How can I bear it? How can I face it alone and with nobody to help me? Oh, God, please find me a way out of this trap!"

# CHAPTER THREE

By the time they reached the battleship at Tilbury which was to carry them through the Mediterranean to the nearest Port to Dūric, Giōna had begun to recover her spirits a little.

She had been desperately unhappy the night before they left, feeling it was impossible for her to leave her mother, Chloris and everything she loved for a strange country and a strange husband, the idea of whom frightened her more every time she thought about him.

From the way the Slavonian Ambassador behaved, and also Captain Darius, she was quite certain that there were things being concealed from her which when she learnt them would prove horrifying.

But as there was nothing she could actually put her finger on, she could not voice her suspicions even to her mother.

Whenever she talked to Chloris, her sister was so relieved that she did not have to give up the man she loved for a throne she did not want that she tried to make everything sound wonderful and predicted for Giōna that it would all be a happy fairy-tale, once she reached Slavonia.

Giōna however was far too intelligent to be deceived.

Because she had adored her father and had attached

herself to him in a way he found very touching, he had talked to her, even when she was quite small, as if she was grown up.

Since he was a very clever and perceptive man, she had learned from him a great deal about people and had developed his natural ability to like and understand them.

She thought things over and knowing that there was nothing she could do to prevent herself from being married to the King and placed on the throne of Slavonia, she decided that if it was within her power she would embellish the position and do what she could to help everybody with whom she came in contact.

But all the time she had the sneaking suspicion that it was not going to be easy, and that there was in fact, although no one would admit it, something strange and perhaps horrifying about the King himself.

It was no use searching through her father's history books for information which she already possessed, and she longed for somebody, preferably Captain Darius, to be frank and tell her exactly what was waiting for her when she arrived in the country over which she was to rule.

But she knew that Captain Darius had in fact spoken the truth when he had said that if the Ambassador or anyone else had the slightest idea that he was doing anything but teaching her the Slavonian language, he would not only be dismissed, but very probably, although it seemed incredible, lose his life.

She was well aware how ruthless the Germans could be when they were up against any type of opposition.

Although the King was Austrian, she had thought it very revealing that he had been brought up in Germany.

By very discreet questioning she learned that although there were a number of Austrians at Court, there were far more Germans and that almost all the Officers in the Slavonian Army were of German origin.

One comfort was that she could not only speak German perfectly, but she was now also becoming very proficient in Slavonian.

She was however careful not to enthuse about it too much to the Ambassador who always questioned her whenever he saw her as to how she was progressing with her studies.

She knew perceptively that he was hoping the answer was not too well.

"It is surprising, Your Royal Highness," he said, "that you have time when you are so busy with your trousseau to continue these lessons which I feel must tax your strength when you have so much else to do."

"I find them interesting, Your Excellency," Giōna replied, "and as you know, my father was very interested in the history of the Balkans, and I know he would not wish me to be ignorant where Slavonia is concerned. There must of course, be in the country many books which have not been translated into other languages."

The Ambassador gave a laugh with no humour in it.

"Books?" he questioned. "I doubt if there is anything you would find particulary interesting considering the Slavonians themselves are an uneducated and, in my opinion, uncivilised lot!"

Giōna did not reply. She knew what he said was untrue.

She had already learned from Captain Darius that the Slavonian poets had already been acclaimed in other countries.

Also they had a culture of their own which, although recently it had been suppressed, was in fact, very interesting to scholars of every nation.

She had challenged him about the word 'suppress'.

"Are you telling me," she enquired, "that your artistic people, like your writers and artists are not encouraged?"

47

Captain Darius had lowered his voice before he replied:

"They are not only discouraged, Your Royal Highness, but wherever it is possible they are prevented from selling their work, whether it is a picture, a book, or a poem outside the country."

"I do not believe it!" Giōna exclaimed.

But she knew that Captain Darius was speaking the truth and not exaggerating.

The three weeks she had been granted to collect her trousseau was coming to an end and the Ambassador was now taking charge, being overbearing and bossy.

He made Giōna feel like a raw recruit being marched up and down a barrack-square.

"It is intolerable, Mama!" she protested to her mother.

Princess Louise merely said:

"Please, darling, do not antagonise him. I agree he is very difficult and a rather tiresome man, but in future you will have to learn to be diplomatic with him and all people like him. It would be a great mistake for you to have adverse reports sent about you to His Majesty."

"If the King and everybody else in Slavonia is going to behave like the Ambassador," Giōna replied, "I shall come home by the next ship. I know I could not bear it!"

Princess Louise had given a cry of horror.

"Please, Giōna, do not talk like that!" she said. "I know, dearest, it is very difficult for you after you have been so happy and free to acclimatise yourself to the restrictions and the repressions of a Court, but it is what every Royal personage has to endure, and there is nothing you can do about it."

"Papa used to say how happy he was when he was a boy and the fun he had with his family."

"That was different," Princess Louise replied, "and I only wish, dearest, that your Papa was with us now, so that he could explain to you how important it is that you should behave in the right way and not upset the King."

Her mother had sounded so unhappy as she spoke that Giōna bit back the words that came to her lips, and knew it was no use complaining when she already knew the answers.

For several nights she cried herself to sleep, and only in the morning did her natural joy of living and her irrepressible vitality make her feel that however bad it was she would somehow not only survive, but win through.

How she was to succeed she was not quite certain. She only felt as if she was fighting a battle on her own against overwhelming odds.

And yet faith and optimism made her feel that eventually everything would come right.

However, although she knew it was very un-Royal to show emotions in public, it was impossible to say goodbye to her mother and Chloris without tears.

Because Princess Louise knew how painful it would be, she had arranged not to accompany her daughter to the ship, but to say goodbye to her in their own home.

When Giōna drove away in a smart carriage loaned by the Queen with the British Ambassador and his wife, her lips were trembling and tears filled her eyes, but with a superhuman effort she prevented them from falling.

Lady Bowden, who was a stout, middle-aged woman, was tactful enough not to talk until they were several miles away, and then to speak of quite ordinary things as if nothing untowards was happening.

Sir Edward was also very diplomatic and as kind as he could possibly be to Giōna.

It was only the Slavonian Ambassador who the moment he got near her talked incessantly and made everything he said sound like a command or instructions on her future behaviour.

It was however a relief to know that they were travel-

49

ling in a British ship with a British crew, and the Captain, when she went aboard, assured her that he would do everything within his power to make the Royal Party as comfortable as possible.

Even so, Giōna heard the Slavonian Ambassador criticising various of the arrangements in a low voice to the other German members of his party, and it made her dislike him more than she did already and try to avoid him as much as possible.

This however was difficult when he deliberately sought her out and at every opportunity tried to convince her that it was a mistake to continue her lessons with Captain Darius.

"As there is a great deal more for me to learn," Giōna replied, "and I have very little time in which to do it, I must insist on not only continuing my lessons, but having them twice a day."

The Slavonian Ambassador spluttered with rage, but Giōna was so firm and spoke with such a new authority that he was obliged to give in to her.

He tried to insist that either Lady Bowden or a member of his staff should chaperon her during her lessons until Giōna said firmly:

"If my mother permitted Captain Darius to teach me without anyone else being present, I cannot believe that it is now necessary simply because we are aboard ship."

The Slavonian Ambassador yielded with a bad grace, but she was certain he would make every effort to listen at the door while her lessons were in progress.

But the moment the ship reached the Bay of Biscay both he and Lady Bowden retired to their cabins and were not seen again until they reached the Mediterranean.

Giōna was in fact, a very good sailor and so was Captain Darius, and they laughed to find that they were almost the only members of the party on their feet.

"At least," Giōna said, as the ship pitched and rolled, "no one will find it possible to keep their ear to the key-hole now, so we can talk without being overheard."

"I know what you are saying to me, Your Royal Highness," Captain Darius replied, "and I beg of you not to tempt me into any indiscretions which later we may both regret."

"I shall never regret knowing the truth," Giōna said, "and I know without your telling me, Captain, that you are apprehensive about what will happen when I reach my new country."

"I have not said so," he said quickly.

"But you think it."

Captain Darius looked at her for a moment before he asked:

"You are too young, too sensitive and too beautiful, Your Royal Highness, to be a political pawn."

"I am aware of that," Giōna said, "at the same time, 'fore-warned is fore-armed', and if I knew what to expect, it would make things a little easier for me."

Captain Darius shook his head.

Because she felt he was not going to tell her what she wanted to know, Giōna said:

"At least explain to me why there is this terrible haste to get me to Slavonia. As you know, most Royal mar-riages in Europe take place after an engagement of at least six months, if not longer."

There was a short pause, then Captain Darius, drawing in his breath, said:

"I cannot believe that you are not aware of the situation in Slavonia at this moment."

"Of course I can guess what it is," Giōna replied sharply, "but you have all contrived to keep it from me from the moment you came to England."

Captain Darius sighed.

"I suppose because it is so important to us, I assumed

it would be known in other countries, and publicised in the newspapers."

"I can honestly say," Giōna answered, "that I have never found anything about Slavonia in the English newspapers, although Mama only takes '*The Morning Post*'."

She bent forward across the table at which they had their lessons and said:

"There cannot be anything wrong in your telling me exactly what the situation is."

"What I say depends on who I say it to, and who overhears it," Captain Darius said with a faint smile.

"Tell me the truth," Giōna begged.

"The truth is quite simple," he said. "Ever since King Ferdinand came to the throne ten years ago, the people have been dissatisfied not only with him as a person, but also because of his insistence on making the country as Germanic as possible."

He smiled before he said:

"The Slavonians are a very simple people. They sing when they are happy, they cry when they are not. They are passionately patriotic, and like all members of Balkan States, are very susceptible to beauty."

He looked at Giōna again as he said:

"That is why they will take Your Royal Highness to their hearts as soon as they see you. It would be impossible for them not to love anybody as lovely as you."

"Thank you," Giōna said, "but tell me the rest."

There seemed to be a long pause before Captain Darius said reluctantly in a voice hardly above a whisper:

"There is a claimant to the throne!"

Giōna's eyes opened wide. This was something she had not at all anticipated.

"A claimant?" she repeated.

"The son of the last King who was considered too young when he died to assume authority, but who is now grown up and old enough to resent a foreigner sitting on the throne which is rightfully his."

Giōna was intrigued.

"That is exciting!" she said. "Tell me more!"

"It is not exciting, Your Royal Highness," Captain Darius contradicted. "In fact, I am being extremely indiscreet in telling you this."

"But you have told me," Giōna insisted, "and now I want to know more. What is the name of this man who is upsetting the King?"

"It is a name that is never spoken!" Captain Darius said surprisingly. "He is known as '*Aoratos*' which means 'The Invisible One' because he is only seen by those who are his people. The King's troops have searched everywhere for him, only to be reprimanded for negligence when they returned to their Barracks empty-handed."

As he spoke Giōna heard a note of elation in his voice which she was sure he was trying to suppress.

"Tell me .. tell me about 'The Invisible One'."

"I really have no more to tell," he said, "but you can understand that the King wants the support of Great Britain, declared of course by your presence as his Queen, in order to prevent a revolution breaking out simply because the Slavonian people want to be ruled by one of their own blood."

"It seems a reasonable idea."

Captain Darius gave a little laugh, but there was no humour in it.

"If you say anything like that to the King, you may have your head chopped off!"

He was teasing her, but Giōna said:

"Perhaps a more pleasant punishment for me would be to be sent back to England in disgrace."

Even as she spoke she knew how upset this would make her mother, and how furious Queen Victoria would be.

She had visions of their being turned out of their Grace

53

and Favour house and the small concession they received from Windsor Castle. Perhaps even her mother's pension would be stopped.

Quickly she said:

"I can only thank you, Captain Darius, for telling me what is happening."

"There is no need for you to be afraid," Captain Darius assured her quickly. "The Palace is guarded very effectively by a large number of troops, and every time the King goes anywhere he is surrounded by so many soldiers that it is almost impossible even to catch a glimpse of him."

There was a sarcastic note in his voice as if he despised the King for being afraid.

Then Giōna, who had been listening wide-eyed, said:

"Is the fact that he is an Austrian the only thing which makes him so unpopular?"

The minute she spoke she saw from the expression in Captain Darius's eyes that she had touched the vital spot with a perceptiveness he had not expected.

To her surprise he hesitated before he said quickly – too quickly:

"That, I am sure, is the only reason, Your Royal Highness," But Giōna knew that he lied.

It was difficult once they reached the calm waters of the Mediterranean for her to have any more frank conversations with Captain Darius.

For one thing, she knew he wished to avoid them, and for another she was quite certain that the Slavonian Ambassador was once again setting his spies on them.

When they were talking in the cabin which they used for her lessons there always seemed to be sounds outside the door, and Giōna had grown too fond of Captain Darius to wish to put him in any danger.

At the same time she overheard several conversations which she thought were very significant.

54

Once she was sitting on deck in the sunshine, when through an open porthole immediately above her head she heard two guttural voices talking in German.

At first she had taken no notice until she heard one say:

"I am sorry for the poor little *Fraulein*. She is far too young and inexperienced to cope with him, and anyway the English dislike that sort of thing."

"I suppose it will be a shock to her," the other man said, "but because she is his wife he may be more restrained where she is concerned."

"I doubt it," the other man said. "He likes them very young, and it will seem lucky to him that he is not being paired off with some elderly Princess whom nobody had previously looked at!"

The other man laughed.

"That is true. At the same time, I am sorry for the child because she is in for a nasty shock!"

"That is what you will have if somebody hears you talking like this," his friend replied. "Come and have a drink. At least there is plenty of that on the ship!"

He walked away laughing and Giōna realised she was clenching her hands together and could hardly breathe while she had been listening to what was being said.

She took a deep breath and wondered frantically what she should do, then knew the answer was – nothing.

Another conversation was one she herself had with Lady Bowden.

By this time they had reached the Ionian Sea and it was only a day or two before they would reach the Port at which they were to disembark.

Giōna, going up on deck in the evening when it was cool, found Lady Bowden sitting in a deck-chair, looking out towards the horizon.

She sat down beside her, saying as she did so:

"I always think the sea looks particularly beautiful just before the sun begins to set."

Lady Bowden looked at her, then she said:

"I agree with you, my dear, and I shall miss the sea once we reach Slavonia. But the mountains there are very lovely and so are the green fields through which a beautiful silver river winds its way through lush meadowland."

"It sounds beautiful and romantic," Giōna agreed.

Lady Bowden paused for a moment before she said:

"I hope, my dear, if there is anything I can ever do to help you in your new position, you will come to me. I know how much you miss your mother, and you will of course feel lonely in a strange country where there are very few English people and at Court few young women of your own age."

Giōna did not say anything and after a moment Lady Bowden went on, choosing her words with care:

"The King will seem to you rather old, as you are so young, but I am sure, as your mother's daughter, you will make every effort to please him and make your marriage compatible."

She gave a sigh before she added:

"I always feel it is the woman who has to do that, and it is not always easy."

"I realise the King is very much older than I am," Giōna said, "so I looked up in the books belonging to Papa to see if there was anybody available older than me. But Her Majesty was right when she told me there was nobody else."

"My husband said the same thing," Lady Bowden replied. "So, dear, you have a very great responsibility on your hands to represent Great Britain and, however strange your life may be, you have to remember that you are British and at this moment of great importance to His Majesty King Ferdinand."

There was a note in her voice which said so much more

56

than the mere formality of her words, and impulsively
Giōna said:

"Tell me the truth, Lady Bowden. What is the King
like as a man? Was his last wife happy with him?"

For a moment Lady Bowden stared at her not only in
surprise, Giōna thought, but almost as if she was afraid.
Then she said:

"You are making it very difficult for me because what
one person finds attractive another may quite easily dislike. The King is a hard man, and I think in many ways
not a very happy one. I am hoping because you are so
pretty that he may fall genuinely in love with you."

"And if he does not?"

"He will – I am sure he will!" Lady Bowden said
quickly.

Then as if she was afraid to say any more she rose
from her deckchair saying:

"I think it is getting a little cold and I should go
below. I have no wish to arrive in Dūric having caught
a chill."

"No, of course not," Giōna agreed.

But she knew the Ambassadress was running away.

. . . . . . .

They docked in a port in the most southerly port of
Albania late one evening, and it was not until the next
morning that the commotion started.

It was then, once Giōna was up and dressed, that a
Slavonian General accompanied by the Foreign Secretary
and a number of other dignitaries came aboard to meet
her.

She received them with the British Ambassador and
Lady Bowden in the Saloon, and although since they were
still on a British ship it was for Sir Edward to take charge
of the proceedings, the Slavonian Ambassador kept
interfering.

There were speeches of welcome, innumerable introduc-

57

tions and, needless to say, the conversation was mainly in English or German.

Apart from Captain Darius, who was ignored by the welcoming party, everybody including the Ministers was, Giōna found, either German or Austrian.

They, however, made a great fuss of her and she was informed that as soon as they were ready the Royal Train was waiting to carry her to Dūric.

It was Lady Bowden who had already told Giōna that the scenery would be very lovely as they travelled through the mountains of Albania for the first part of the journey.

They came into Slavonia through a mountainous pass, after which the train would descend down to Dūric, about a four-hour run from the frontier to the Capital.

"Unfortunately, however," she had added, "as the route up through the mountains is very slow, we shall have to spend one night on the train. But I think Your Royal Highness will be very comfortable because you will have His Majesty's private coach which he designed himself."

As Giōna had never travelled on a private train before, she was looking forward to it, and she was, she knew, in no hurry to reach Dūric and face the King.

They did not leave the ship until after an early luncheon at which the visitors ate, she thought, an inordinate amount, and expressed their appreciation not only in words but with an occasional hiccup as they left with the ship's Band playing and were carried away from the Quay in numerous carriages to the railway station.

Here again there was more ceremony as they were received by the Mayor of the Port and several Town Councillors before Giōna was finally allowed to enter the Royal Carriage.

It was, as she expected, very comfortable, and regally decorated with crimson velvet and heavy Persian carpets.

There was a Drawing-Room which was large enough to seat eight to ten people in comfort, and out of it a bedroom.

This took up half the carriage and could only have been designed for a man. There was oak panelling, a carved mahogany bedstead, and everything fitted neatly around the walls without, from a woman's point of view, there being enough mirrors and enough light to see one's self properly.

Here too the curtains over the windows were of crimson velvet, the carpet was crimson, and so was the bedspread embellished with the King's Insignia which were also echoed on the bedhead.

'His Majesty certainly makes sure that everybody is aware that he is Royal!' Giōna thought to herself, but she did not say it aloud.

As the train started she took off her bonnet helped by a maid who informed her in very badly spoken German that she was there to help her.

She was an attractive woman of perhaps thirty or more and after a moment Giōna said:

"I think, if I am not mistaken, that you are a Slavonian."

She spoke in the same language and the woman's eyes lit up.

"You speak our language, Your Royal Highness!"

"I have been learning it all the while I have been coming here," Giōna said.

"But that is marvellous! It's indeed a miracle! No one has ever talked to me in my own language ever since I've been at the Palace."

"How long is that?" Giōna enquired.

"Over five years, Your Royal Highness."

"Then you must help me to become more proficient," Giōna said. "Will you be looking after me when I arrive?"

"That's what I hope, Your Royal Highness, but it depends on whether it pleases you."

"It pleases me very much that you are Slavonian," Giōna said.

She chatted away to her for some time, then went into the Drawing-Room to where the Bowdens and the Slavonian Ambassador were waiting for her.

She had already learnt that there was a second coach attached to this one, and she was relieved that she would be alone and not have to listen to them chattering in the Drawing-Room if she wished to go to bed.

Almost as if she was aware of what Giōna was thinking Lady Bowden asked:

"Do you mind being alone, Your Royal Highness? His Excellency was just saying that if you are nervous, either your lady's-maid or one of the *Aides-de-Camp* could be on duty at night here in the Drawing-Room."

Giōna laughed.

"I should hate that! I am sure they would keep me awake either by coughing or moving about, and I would much prefer to be alone. I am not in the least worried, I assure you."

"We are only one door away, so to speak, if you need us," Lady Bowden said. "When His Majesty designed the carriage he said he very much disliked having servants too near to him, whether they were senior or junior, and therefore insisted upon having a coach entirely to himself."

"I am sure he was right," Giōna said. "It would be a great mistake for outsiders to know whether one snored or not!"

She meant what she said as a joke, but the Slavonian Ambassador looked shocked as though she had committed *lèse-majesté* in suggesting that the King snored.

Because she wanted to see the countryside, Giōna deliberately sat on the opposite side of the Drawing-

Room from the others so that she could look out of the window.

After she had answered them in monosyllables for a little while they gave up trying to talk to her, and while the two Ambassadors conversed together in low tones, Lady Bowden dozed.

Later they stopped at a station and dinner was brought into the carriage where they were joined by the Senior Ministers for what was a long-drawn-out, rather heavy meal which Giōna found extremely boring, although she chided herself for thinking so.

Captain Darius was of course not included in the party and everyone else, she decided, was well over fifty.

Although they occasionally appeared to remember her presence and made desultory remarks which were so banal that she could hardly bother to answer them, the rest of the time they talked amongst themselves.

They talked of things about which she knew nothing and which she was sure would purposely not reveal to her anything she might wish to know.

At last, when she felt it impossible not to yawn and the port and liqueurs had been passed around the table at least half-a-dozen times, the train came to a standstill.

The Slavonian Ambassador rose to draw back one of the velvet curtains and exclaimed:

"The Manski Pass! Well, that was quick! I had no idea we should get here so soon."

Because it had seemed to Giōna an inordinately long time, she thought it could only have been the food and the drink that had made the time seem to them to pass quickly.

She was therefore thankful when Lady Bowden said:

"I think now we should retire to our own quarters and allow Her Royal Highness to get some sleep. She has a long day in front of her tomorrow."

"That is true," the Slavonian Ambassador replied. "We

61

shall be leaving, Your Royal Highness, at eight o'clock, and we will arrive in the Capital just before luncheon. His Majesty will be waiting impatiently to meet you, and with him will be the Prime Minister and other Members of the Government."

He paused before he added:

"You may have to say a few words, but I doubt it. I am sure His Majesty will thank everybody for their congratulations for you, and all you will have to do is to smile at him and receive everyone with dignity and, I am sure, pleasure."

Once again he was talking as if she was a raw recruit and Giōna longed to tell him so. But instead she said quietly:

"Thank you for telling me, and now, as Her Ladyship has suggested, I am tired and I should be grateful if my maid could be sent to me to help me to bed."

After that there was nothing anyone could do but leave, and she thought several of the Ministers looked reluctantly at the wine which was still on the table.

However servants arrived to carry it away and soon, after quite an unnecessary number of goodnights, she was alone.

She pulled back the curtains from one of the windows and saw they were, as she had expected, high up in the mountains and she could see the peaks of one silhouetted against the stars.

Then her maid, whose name was Mithra, came hurrying into the carriage saying as she did so:

"Your Royal Highness must be tired. It's very late."

"How late?" Giōna enquired.

"Nearly midnight, Your Royal Highness."

Giōna sighed.

"I thought it must be, but nobody wanted to stop drinking."

Mithra laughed.

"That's what we always say about the Germans," she said. "Drink! Drink! Drink!"

Then as if she felt she had been indiscreet she put her hand across her lips.

"I'm sorry, Your Royal Highness, I should not have said that!"

"Let me make it clear from the beginning," Giōna said, "that if you are going to look after me, and I hope you will, we will be frank with each other. It would be a mistake if you had to worry over every word in case you say something indiscreet. I want you to say what you like, Mithra, and I shall enjoy that, I like frankness, and if I should speak to you in a very frank way, I know you will not repeat it."

To her surprise Mithra went down on one knee and raised her hands to her lips.

"You're a very lovely lady, Your Royal Highness, just as I felt an English lady would be. I'm very, very proud to serve you."

"Thank you," Giōna said rather touched. "And now, Mithra, come and help me undress because otherwise I shall be alseep when we leave at eight o'clock."

They went into the bedroom and Giōna took off the pretty gown she had put on for dinner.

Mithra helped her into her nightgown and a satin negligée which she had thought she might need if they were stopping in the mountains.

But it was not nearly as cold as she had expected, and she was certain that tomorrow would be very hot down in the valley when they reached Dūric.

She had already decided what she would wear for her first appearance in her new country.

She knew all the gowns her mother had chosen for her were in perfect taste and, because they could afford to be extravagant, since the Queen was paying, very attractive.

Mithra brushed Giōna's hair as it fell over her shoulders

until it danced with the electricity from the height at which they had stopped.

Then with a low curtsy Mithra said:

"Is there anything else I can do for Your Royal Highness?"

"Nothing, thank you," Giōna replied.

She had already said she did not wish to get into bed for the moment, because she intended when she was alone to look out of the windows at the mountains and say her prayers while she was looking at them.

She almost felt as if they would be more effective here at this height than if she said them by her bed.

"Then I will say goodnight, Your Royal Highness," Mithra said, "and may the angels guard you."

"I am sure they will do that," Giōna replied, "and perhaps I shall need the protection of the angels tomorrow in case 'The Invisible One' strikes at me!"

She spoke deliberately because she wondered what Mithra, because she was a Slavonian, would say.

But she was not prepared for the look of horror that came over the woman's face or the fact that she put her hands up in an instinctive gesture to her breasts as if to quell the shock that Giōna's words had given her.

"What does – Your Royal Highness – know of – 'The Invisible One'?" she asked hesitatingly after a moment.

"Very little," Giōna replied, "and I would like you to tell me what you know."

Mithra looked absolutely horrified.

"To speak of him in the privacy of His Majesty's carriage is dangerous, very, very dangerous, Your Royal Highness. Another day, another time, but not here!"

She made a little sound that was one of sheer terror and crossed herself, then she curtsied again before she slipped out through the bedroom door and Giōna heard her running across the Drawing-Room and out beyond it to the entrance of the Royal Coach.

64

She was aware that since they had come to a standstill a set of wooden steps had been set outside the coach for the convenience of those who wished to enter or leave it.

Now on either side of the steps stood a sentry.

Giōna stood where Mithra had left her, thinking how strange the woman's behaviour was. But she noted with satisfaction that she knew about 'The Invisible One', and there was therefore a chance that sooner or later she would be able to learn something from her.

"It is all like a story in a novel," she told herself.

She was about to pull back the curtains of her bedroom when she realised that if she did so anyone outside would be able to see her.

Instead she opened the door and went into the Drawing-Room.

Here there was only one small light left burning and this she extinguished before she drew back the curtains and looked out.

She could see the rocky sides of the Pass, the trees growing above them, and higher still the mountains, impressive and beautiful against the stars.

It was however a rather limited view from the windows and she could not see as high as she would have liked.

Although she knew it was imprudent to do so, she walked down the Drawing-Room into the small passage-way and opened the door which led onto the rough ground because there was no platform on what she guessed was the top of the Pass.

The two sentries who had been close against the steps earlier in the evening had now moved a little further away, but were still standing at attention, their rifles in their hands, their backs to her.

They were protecting her, she thought with a faint smile, from the rocks and the trees, for there was nothing else to be seen.

She stood in the doorway of the carriage and now she

had a magnificent view, not only of the peaks just above her, but also of the other peaks in the distance.

The stars shone like diamonds in the sable sky and a young moon was rising to throw its silver light on the stoney sides of the mountain-tops.

It was all so lovely that Giōna drew in her breath.

It was what she had expected and she knew now it would be easy to pray for what she wanted, feeling somehow she was nearer to God than she had been at any other time since she had left England.

At that moment there was a loud and violent explosion somewhere towards the front of the train.

It was about six carriages away, but in the silence of the night the noise seemed deafening and as Giōna stared from where she was standing, finding it impossible to see anything as the train curved slightly away from her to the right, there was the sound of firing and the two sentries lifted their rifles to hold them at the ready.

It appeared to come from the engine, but from where she stood it was difficult to see.

Doors were opening and soldiers were jumping out onto the ground.

There was a return of fire and the two sentries were watching what was happening.

Giōna was just about to ask them what was occurring when suddenly there came a whisper from below her feet and to her astonishment a man's voice speaking in English said:

"Save me! For God's sake save me!"

# CHAPTER FOUR

Afterwards Giōna was to realise that she acted instantaneously by sheer instinct rather than by making any conscious decision.

With hardly a pause she walked down the steps towards the sentries and when she was within a few feet of them she stopped and said:

"I think there was a movement in those bushes. I am sure I saw somebody there."

She spoke as she pointed to a clump of bushes about twenty yards away by the rail-side.

As she anticipated the sentries hurried forward, and as they did so she was certain without turning her head that somebody slipped up the steps and into her coach.

She was just about to turn and go back when running from the end of the train came a number of soldiers led by an officer.

They were carrying fixed bayonets and the officer, holding a pistol in his hand, came hastily to a stop when he realised who she was.

"Are you all right, Your Royal Highness?" he asked in German.

"Perfectly, thank you, Major," Giōna replied, knowing his rank from the insignia on his shoulder.

The Officer glanced to where the sentries were inspecting somewhat warily the bushes Giōna had pointed out to them.

As if he asked the question, she said:

"I thought I saw a movement in those shrubs."

The Officer without hesitation, gave the word of command and his men followed him swiftly towards the bushes.

Giōna climbed back up the steps and into her coach.

Only as she went in through the door did she wonder if she had done something reprehensible, and perhaps even dangerous.

Then she remembered the plea for help had been spoken in English, and she shut the door behind her and bolted it.

As she turned to enter the Drawing-Room she realised it was in complete darkness.

Somebody had closed the curtains which she had left open so that she could look at the stars.

For a moment she was frightened, then a voice, very low and deep, said in English:

"Do not be afraid – I will not harm you, and I am very grateful."

The voice came from the far end of the Drawing-Room as Giōna put out her hands in front of her to feel her way and sat down in the first chair she found.

There was silence, then before she could speak came the sound of shots outside.

She was not certain whether they came from the end of the train where the explosion had taken place, or from the bushes where she had sent the sentries and the other soldiers.

She knew as she listened that the man in the Drawing-Room with her was also listening as intently as she was.

Then in a voice which quivered a little because she was beginning to feel frightened, Giōna asked:

"What is happening?"

68

"You do not know?"

"No one has told me anything."

She had the feeling that the man to whom she was speaking was thinking before he replied:

"A bomb was thrown at the engine which was intended to prevent it from travelling any further."

"Who threw it?" Giōna asked.

"What you would call 'revolutionaries'," was the answer, "but I would refer to as 'patriots'."

"You mean you are Slavonian?"

"Exactly!"

"You are Slavonian and yet you speak English!"

"Would you have preferred me to speak in German?"

Giōna smiled.

"I can speak your language also," she said.

The man gave an exclamation.

"That is good! You have taken the trouble to learn the language of this country! That is certainly something nobody would have expected you to do."

Before Giōna could reply there was the sound of voices outside the coach and she heard somebody try to open the door.

When they realised it was bolted they knocked loudly.

She felt her heart give a frightened leap and was aware that the man she could not see in the darkness was tense.

How she knew this she was not certain, except that she was aware of his vibrations and they were very strong.

She deliberately waited for several seconds, then as the knock came again she said, knowing that whoever was outside would suppose she had come from the bedroom to the door:

"Who is it?"

"It is Colonel Muller, Your Royal Highness. I have been sent by His Excellency to ask if you are all right. He would have come at once himself, but he had already retired for the night when the explosion happened. However he is dressing and should be with you shortly."

Giōna drew in her breath and said:

"Please, thank His Excellency for his concern, but I am perfectly all right. As I am tired, I have no wish to see anyone."

"His Excellency thinks, Your Royal Highness, that you should have a member of his staff in your Drawing-Room to guard you during the night."

"There is no need for that," Giōna said firmly, "although it is very gracious of His Excellency to think of it. Inform him that I am now going to sleep and do not want to be awakened again."

"You are quite certain, Your Royal Highness, that you would not like somebody to be with you?"

"Quite certain," Giōna insisted. "Goodnight Colonel and thank you!"

As she did not hear the Colonel move away she knew that he was upset at her decision, and wanted to continue to argue that she should have somebody on guard in the Drawing-Room.

But after a while, as if he knew he could do nothing but accept her decision, she heard him walk down the wooden steps and away towards the front of the train.

The man in the darkness gave a low laugh.

"You were very firm with him. Do you always get your own way?"

"Not very often," Giōna admitted.

There was the sound of footsteps outside and of soldiers coming to a halt.

"I think, after all, you have a body-guard outside," the man said.

"I am afraid so," Giōna replied, "which means we must talk very quietly, or else they will think I am mad and talking to myself!"

"I am very honoured that you intend to talk to me,"

was the reply, "and may I suggest, if it will not make you nervous, that we draw a little closer to each other?"

"I was already thinking that," Giōna said. "If we go to the other side of this compartment, it will be harder for them to overhear us."

She rose as she spoke and moved through the furniture feeling her way to the other side of the small Drawing-Room.

As she reached the window she realised the man she had rescued was very near to her, but as they sat down in two chairs facing each other, Giōna was aware she was not frightened.

In fact, although it seemed strange, she trusted him.

"Now, please," she said in a murmured whisper, "tell me exactly what has happened and who you are."

"I will tell you what was intended to happen," he said, "if it will not upset you."

Again he was speaking in English. Then as he hesitated wondering where to begin Giōna gave a little cry.

"I know who you are!" she said. "You are 'The Invisible One'!"

She was aware that he stiffened before he asked:

"What do you know about 'The Invisible One'?"

"Only that everybody is frightened to speak of him, but he is in fact, the Pretender to the Throne of Slavonia."

There was silence, and as the man opposite her did not speak she said:

"That is true, is it not?"

"I am astonished, completely astonished," was the answer, "because I did not expect you to be aware of what was happening here in my country. I cannot believe that His Excellency, the most esteemed Ambassador of Slavonia, would have been so frank!"

He spoke with a sarcastic note in his voice that made Giōna want to laugh, and she answered:

"No, you may be certain it was not him, but somebody else."

She wondered if he would guess that it was Captain Darius, but as she had no wish to say anything which might hurt the young Slavonian she said:

"Please, in case you vanish and I never know the truth, tell me exactly what has happened, and why the Royal Train was attacked."

"It was intended," the man opposite her replied, "that it should be burned to the ground with everybody in it!"

Giōna gave a gasp of horror. Then she said in a voice that trembled:

"You mean the .. men you call .. patriots .. wanted to .. destroy me?"

"They want to destroy anything that would uphold the present *Régime* which is what you have been brought here to do," the man opposite her replied.

"Then .. what happened? Why have they .. not carried out .. their intention?"

"I was in the other side of the valley, quite some way from here," the man answered, "and I only learned at the last moment what had been planned. I arrived too late to prevent the bomb from being thrown into the engine, but I was able to prevent the rest of the train from being set on fire. Unfortunately in doing so I was very nearly captured, and I can never be sufficiently grateful to you, Princess, for saving my life."

"If they had caught you, what would have happened?"

"I would have been shot and there would have been no chance to explain that I did not intend to destroy you."

There was a long pause. Then Giōna asked:

"Why did you .. wish to save me?"

"I do not wish to wage war on a girl who is too young to know what she is doing."

There was a note of scorn in the voice which made Giōna ask curiously:

72

"Is that the only reason why you saved me?"

"The newspapers of Slavonia have carried stories about you for the last two weeks, extolling your beauty and explaining how young you were. Much, much too young to be the wife of King Ferdinand. Whatever made you agree to such a marriage?"

The man in the dark spoke sternly and before Giōna could reply he added in a voice that he had not used before:

"But of course! What woman could resist a throne?"

"It is not that! Of course it is not that!" Giōna said angrily.

"You did not wish to be a Queen?"

"Not with a King almost old enough to be my grandfather! Nor do I wish to be married to any man I do not love."

"Love?" the man opposite her enquired. "Are you suggesting that love is to be found in any Royal marriage?"

"My father and mother were deeply in love with each other," Giōna said. "They had some difficulty in marrying because Papa was only the younger son of a King without a Kingdom, but they loved each other very much, and .. Mama has never been the same since my father died."

There was something rather touching in her voice, and after a moment the man in the dark said very quietly:

"And that was the love you hoped to find?"

"Of course I did! My sister has been very lucky. She has found a man she loves and who loves her. If I had not agreed to come to Slavonia, or had run away and hidden myself where they could not find me, as I thought at first of doing, then Chloris would have been forced to come. She was the Queen's first choice."

"I can understand what happened," the man in the dark said. "At the same time, it is wrong, wicked that

73

you should be sent out here without the slightest idea of what to expect or what marriage to a man who is – so much older will – entail."

He hesitated over the last few words and Giōna had the feeling he had been about to say something very different.

"But I am here now," she said in a very small voice, "and there is nothing I can do but marry the King, as has been arranged."

She heard the man opposite draw in his breath in an exasperated manner, as if even the thought of it made him angry.

Because she had the feeling that time was passing and there was so much more she wished to know, she said quickly:

"Please tell me more about what is happening. It is frightening to be so ignorant and have everything kept from me. How strong are the patriots?"

She thought for a moment he was not going to answer. Then he said:

"As strong as it is possible to be without the money with which to buy new weapons."

"And would it really be best for the country if they were in power rather than the present King?" Giōna asked.

She knew the answer to that, but she wanted to hear him say it.

Once again she heard him draw in his breath as if he felt she had given him a difficult task.

"How much do you know of the situation in the Balkans at the present moment?"

"Very little," Giōna admitted. "When Papa was alive I knew a great deal because he was so interested in all the Balkan countries and we used to talk about it together. But the English newspapers never seem to mention any except the great powers, and because we are poor and live very quietly in a Grace and Favour house at Windsor we are not very well informed."

"Then I must try to explain it to you," the man opposite her said. "In 1872 the League of the three Emperors was formed by which the Austrian, German and Russian Emperors agreed to work together to preserve peace. It is only now, three years later, that we in Slavonia have realised that their idea of peace was to incorporate all the independent countries of the Balkans into the Austro-Hungarian Empire, which is dominated by Germany."

Giōna gave a little gasp.

"Is that really true?"

"I promise you, the Balkan countries are losing their independence one by one, and Slavonia will, in a very short time, be completely Austrianised – or Germanised – whatever you wish to call it."

"I .. do not understand," Giōna said. "If that is so, why has the King agreed to take a British Queen?"

"He was forced into agreeing by the Slavonian Party in the House of Parliament. It was also thought by most of the population to be the only possible way of saving the country from being overrun.

"The newspapers have been saying for over a year that only Britain can save Slavonia, and there have been mass meetings, urgent representations, even riots, bringing pressure to bear on the King to carry out their wishes."

Giōna did not speak and after a moment the man opposite her added:

"It meant that eventually the King had to agree or else face an outright war or revolution such as is happening in other parts of the Balkans."

"I see .. now I understand."

"There are also some of our number," the man went on, "who believe that the marriage will strengthen the King in his position on the throne, and it is they who wished to destroy you, rather than allow you to bolster up a Monarchy they hate and despise."

"Because he is Austrian?" Giōna asked.

"There are other reasons."

"What are they?"

"I see no point in discussing it. I have saved your life and you have saved mine, and now I should leave you. I can only hope you will find some happiness in the future."

The way he spoke made Giōna think that in his opinion this was very unlikely and she said impulsively:

"I am frightened! I think I am more frightened now of being married to a strange old man than I was even when I left England."

"I can understand that," the man in the darkness said. "At the same time, you may save Slavonia from being gobbled up as other countries have been."

"I will try to do what is right for your Slavonia," Giōna replied, "but I know it will be very difficult."

"Too difficult," the man said sharply, "and much too hard for somebody young like yourself. You should be happy and free and not just a political pawn."

"That is what I thought myself," Giōna answered, "but there was nothing I could do but agree to what the Queen proposed."

"I do not suppose that she or anybody else in England had any idea of what you would encounter when you arrived here."

The man spoke in a low voice, as if he was speaking to himself rather than to Giōna, and she gave a little cry saying:

"What do you mean? What is being kept from me? I know there is something but no one will be honest with me. I would much rather face facts than imagine with terror something perhaps worse than what I shall actually discover."

The man opposite her suddenly said:

"Give me your hand."

Without thinking Giōna stretched hers out and he took

76

them in both of his.

"Listen to me, Princess," he said. "You saved my life with a courage and quick thinking that I would not have believed possible in any young woman, and since we have talked together here in the darkness, I know you are everything a Queen should be, and the people of my country when they know you, will give you their hearts."

His fingers tightened on hers as he said:

"But I will not disguise the fact that there are great difficulties ahead, and I want you to promise me that if you find them too taxing and in fact unbearable, you will ask me to help you. I do not know how, but if it be possible, I swear that I will try by every means in my power to save you."

He spoke so solemnly that Giōna could only sit wide-eyed in the darkness.

At the same time she was acutely conscious that the vibrations that came from him and from his hands as he touched hers seemed almost electric, as if everything about him was more alive than in anyone she had ever known.

As he finished speaking, she said in a very small, very young voice:

"Thank you. I feel somehow . . happier because I know . . you are . . there."

She paused. Then she asked:

"You will not forget me?"

She was sure he smiled before he replied:

"That would be impossible!"

He bent his head and she felt his lips on the softness of her skin.

"Now I must go."

"How can you do that?" Giōna asked. "The sentries will still be outside."

"I know that," he said, "but if you will permit me to go into your bedroom, there is a trap-door in the floor through which I can let myself down onto the line, and they will not see me."

"Supposing they do?"

"Then I shall be shot, as I would have been a little while ago, if you had not rescued me."

"Please, please, take care of yourself," Giōna begged.

"I will do that," he replied, "not only because you have asked me to, but because I believe at this moment I am necessary to Slavonia."

He stood up as he spoke. Then when he would have moved away in the darkness she said:

"Supposing I do need you? How can I get in touch? How shall I know where to find you?"

"Send me a message by any Slavonian you can trust."

"Shall I tell them it is for 'The Invisible One'?"

"Of course! They will understand, and because I admire you, my little Princess, if I am alive, God willing, I will save you."

He stood still after he had spoken and Giōna had a strange feeling that he was looking at her in the darkness and could see her, while she could not see him.

Then with a faint sigh he turned away towards her bedroom door.

"Wait here," he said, "and pray that I shall reach those who will be waiting for me."

"I will pray very hard," Giōna said, "and God go with you."

It was something she had never said in her life before, and yet the words seemed to come naturally to her lips.

He turned away, opened her bedroom door, and for a moment she saw him silhouetted against the light.

He was tall with broad shoulders and what she fancied was a slim, athletic body.

Then the door closed behind him.

She did not move as she began praying.

There was no sound from the bedroom but she supposed he was raising the rugs under which there would be a trap-door just large enough for a man to enter or leave the compartment.

Now she guessed that the man to whom she had been speaking was lowering himself down onto the rails beneath the train and moving silently and swiftly.

Then he would slip away between the shrubs and rocks on the other side of it without being detected.

And yet there was always the fear that some soldier alert to every shadow and movement in the darkness, would fire at him.

"Please, God, save him!" Giōna prayed.

Clasping her hands together she felt her prayer wing its way up to Heaven through the stars, while with every nerve in her body she was listening in case there came the sound of a shot and the cry of a man as he died.

Only a long time later, when she knew 'The Invisible One' must by now have got away, did she rise and go into her bedroom.

As she expected, one of the rugs in the centre of the floor at the end of the bed was turned back and she could see the trap-door beneath it which had been closed by the man who had passed through it.

She pulled the rug back in place, then taking off her satin negligée she got into bed.

By now it was very late, in fact early in the morning and she knew that soon the stars would begin to fade and the first pale fingers of the dawn would sweep away the brightness of the moon.

By then 'The Invisible One' would be far away and, she hoped, safe.

Before she fell asleep she found herself praying that he had spoken the truth when he had said he would not forget her.

. . . . . . .

The following morning she was awakened to learn that there would be some delay before they could move on.

The engine had been severely damaged by the explosion and another had been sent from the Capital to bring their train to where the King and the Civic Representatives were waiting to receive her.

Mithra was horrified at what had happened during the night and shocked that Her Royal Highness should have been disturbed by the explosion and the shots.

At the same time Giōna had the feeling that the maid knew perfectly well who the aggressors were, and sympathised with them.

It was the Ambassador and Sir Edward when they came to breakfast in the Drawing-Room who spoke up against the revolutionaries, saying their behaviour was disgraceful and the King would undoubtedly take far stronger measures to keep them under control than he had done in the past.

"If we had not had so many soldiers to guard us, we might all have been murdered in our beds!" Lady Bowden said with a shiver. "I cannot understand why, in the face of such a large Army, these people are able to cause so much trouble."

"It has been difficult to catch them, My Lady," a member of the staff said. "One Slavonian looks like another Slavonian, and how can we know that the man pushing a cart through the streets has not a bomb hidden under the vegetables he is pretending to sell, or the old crossing-sweeper has not a pistol in his pocket?"

"You are frightening Her Royal Highness," Sir Edward said firmly, "and I think such a thing is a mistake, especially at breakfast-time."

"I agree with you," the Slavonian Ambassador said, "but I assure you that, when I relate to His Majesty what has happened, he will set in train some stronger and more unpleasant reprisals for the outrage that was perpetrated upon us last night."

Because it was something she had been longing to know

80

but been afraid to ask, Giōna enquired:

"Were many people killed?"

"Two of our soldiers were badly wounded," the Slavonian Ambassador replied, "and I know a number of the revolutionaries were injured, although when they escaped in the darkness they took their wounded with them."

Giōna said nothing. She wondered what they would think if she told them she had spent at least an hour with the leader of the revolutionaries – 'The Invisible One'.

Finally the replacement engine arrived and having been attached to the train drew them off, descending as rapidly as possible, and at last Giōna could see the countryside and realised it was even more beautiful than she had expected.

High mountains, many of them with snow on their highest peaks, encircled the valley which broadened out far and wide beneath them.

Through it ran the wide silver river twisting its way through the land luxuriant with pasture and blossoming trees, and dotted with small hamlets in which most of the white houses had attractive red roofs.

It was so lovely that she longed to talk about it to her father and ask him if there was any country in the whole of the Balkans that was as pretty as Slavonia.

When they passed the people who stood staring in awe and admiration at the train, she saw that they looked very attractive, many of the women being quite beautiful and the men broad shouldered and strong.

They appeared to Giōna to be a smiling people, and as if they realised who the train carried, they waved as it passed them and she waved back.

It was after luncheontime when finally they drew up at the station of Dūric.

There were flags everywhere, the flags of Slavonia side by side with the Union Jack, and the whole station was decorated with flowers.

Standing on a red carpet, waiting for the coach which contained Giōna to come to a standstill, was a mass of civic dignitaries, besides a number of officers festooned with medals, and one man in the centre wearing a plumed hat, who she was certain at first glance, was the King.

For a moment she felt she could not look at him. Then she told herself to be sensible and behave as her mother would expect her to.

She had a wild impulse to run away and hide and say she could not go on with this farce of a marriage.

Then she lifted her chin and told herself that she would not be intimidated by anyone, even a fifty-two year old King, and as she was Royal she would not show emotion.

It was some consolation to know that her mother had chosen for her arrival a lovely and very expensive gown of forget-me-not blue, trimmed with lace threaded by blue ribbons, and ornamented with tiny musk roses.

She looked very young and very lovely as she stepped down from the train onto the red-carpeted platform.

"Let me welcome you to my country," the King said in English and his guttural voice sounded a little hoarse. "We welcome you with our hearts, and I and my people will strive for your happiness."

It flashed through Giōna's mind that the speech had been written for the King because he hesitated over one word, and she knew perceptively that he was trying to remember it rather than it coming spontaneously to his lips.

It was what she might have expected. Then as she looked at him she was aware that it was not that he was so old which made him somehow repulsive, but that there was something hard, almost cruel, in the sharp line of his lips and the cold speculation in his eyes.

She quickly made a speech in German which she had written out for her mother to approve and which she had learned by heart.

"I thank Your Majesty for your most kind and generous welcome. I am very happy to be here in your lovely country where I hope to make my home, and I am certain I will grow to love it in the same way as I love England."

If the King was pleased at her response he did not say so. He merely introduced her rather sharply to the other men standing beside him on the platform.

There were no women, Giōna noticed, but there was the Prime Minister and many Ministers of State, besides half-a-dozen Generals and Councillors with heavy gold chains around their necks which seemed to weigh them down.

They all wished to say something pleasant to Giōna, but the King was obviously very impatient.

"Come along, come along!" he said in German moving her forward. "Everything is late, although it could not be prevented, and we must now make up for lost time."

Giōna wondered what was the hurry, but there was no chance of asking questions before she found herself in an open Landau, driving beside the King to the cheers of the populace which lined the streets.

She waved at them but noticed that the King made no effort from his side of the carriage to even raise his hand.

Instead he sat rather stiffly staring at the crowd as if he was looking for an assassin.

There was certainly a great number of soldiers lining the route, and the horses drove at a quick pace which made Giōna feel that the people, who must have waited for many hours to see her, were not getting their money's worth.

She was however, too nervous to suggest to the King that they should go slower, but merely redoubled her efforts to wave as she passed, hoping they would see from her smile how gratified she was by their reception.

As the Palace came in sight the King spoke for the first time since they had left the station.

"There is no need to overdo it! They wanted an English Queen, and now they have one!"

Giōna looked at him in surprise and asked:

"And did you not want one?"

"Of course! Of course!" the King said sharply. "And I am very pleased to see you!"

She thought however that he did not seem very enthusiastic and imagined perhaps he was feeling embarrassed as she was.

The Palace was a large building, erected several centuries earlier, standing high above the City in what Giōna knew would be beautiful gardens.

There was a long flight of steps up to the front door and as she started up them on the red carpet the King walked beside her in silence not offering her his arm as she would have expected in the circumstances.

Just inside the Palace were standing another large group of people to be introduced, which the King did quickly obviously wishing to waste no more time on pleasantries.

Then they were in a large and very impressive Ante-Room which led into the Dining-Room.

"There is no time for titivating!" the King said quickly. "As everything has been delayed for two hours, you will eat as you are."

Because he spoke in such an authoritative tone, Giōna longed to say she would wish at least to remove her bonnet and wash her hands.

But she had the feeling that he would be extremely annoyed if she said anything of the sort.

As soon as the guests who had followed them from the station arrived, they moved hurriedly into the Dining-Room where more guests were already waiting for them.

There were no introductions, but they clapped as Giōna appeared.

She tried to smile and bow as she walked quickly beside the King to their seats at the top of the table.

They sat down side by side and after a Bishop had said Grace, the King asked:

"What happened last night? I have every intention of finding the culprits, and also punishing those whose duty it was to bring the train through the Pass in safety. It is disgraceful, utterly disgraceful, that you should be greeted in such a manner the moment you arrive in this country!"

"There is no real harm done," Giōna said, "and really I think it would be a good idea to forget it."

"Forget it?" the King demanded sharply. "I have never heard such nonsense! If you give these people an inch they will take a mile! They have been behaving outrageously lately, and I will not stand for it! They are going to learn that I have no intention of putting up with their nonsense!"

He spoke in a harsh, authoritative voice that seemed to ring out round the table and for a moment there was silence as everybody near them looked at him apprehensively before the King went on:

"God knows what will happen if we cannot step out of our own front doors without being attacked and having bombs thrown at us! It is up to those who guard us to see that such atrocities do not occur."

He glared at the General who was sitting three seats away from him at the table, and although he was a large, rather impressive figure, Giōna felt he seemed to crumble before the King's gaze and his red face visibly paled.

"Are you listening to what I am saying, General?" the King demanded.

"I assure Your Majesty everything will be done to bring these malefactors to justice."

"So I should hope! So I should hope!" the King said. "The whole thing is completely disgraceful! Apart from anything else, it made us late for luncheon!"

When the food did arrive it was very heavy and, Giōna thought, Germanic.

There was a great amount of meat which the King, as well as his guests, ate with relish, preceded by fish in pastry and followed by puddings covered with cream.

What Giōna enjoyed was the fish, which she guessed must have come from the silver river, and the vegetables which were different from anything she had eaten in England.

She refused the wine, never when at home having been allowed to drink anything but water, except occasionally at Christmas or some other Festival.

She noticed a number of different wines were served, which the guests drank with appreciation and their glasses were filled and refilled.

The luncheon was long-drawn-out and continued as course succeeded course and one wine followed another, until Giōna was sure it must be teatime.

Then there were speeches by the Prime Minister who welcomed her to Slavonia, the Lord Chief Justice, and a number of other extremely dull gentlemen who apparently had no idea when it was a good thing to sit down.

Naturally it was all in German, and it was lucky, Giōna thought, that she could understand that language. At the same time she had never thought it at all an attractive one.

She wished she could hear Slavonian, which she had learnt from Captain Darius was very soft and attractive, with some words sounding poetical just in themselves.

She was feeling rather exhausted when at last the luncheon came to an end, and Lady Bowden came to her side to introduce her to some of the ladies, although there were not many of them, who had been in the luncheon party.

At long last, when Giōna thought there was nothing

left to say, she was allowed to go to her bedroom where to her relief she found Mithra waiting for her.

"You must be tired, Your Royal Highness," the maid said solicitously.

"I am indeed," Giōna replied. "I have never heard so many long speeches and so many words saying the same thing over and over again."

She laughed as she spoke and Mithra said:

"It is always the same: the Austrian and the Germans they talk and they drink. Sometimes they sing, although not in the Palace!"

Giōna looked around at the room and thought it was very ugly, but she supposed it was only temporary accommodation until she was married, when she would move into a more important State Bedroom.

As if Mithra knew what she was thinking she said:

"Before I was here I believe the Palace was very lovely, but now the curtains over the beds have been taken away and many of the beautiful pictures are now stacked in the attics."

"Why is that?" Giōna asked.

"His Majesty thinks such frivolities unnecessary and a waste of time."

Giōna laughed.

She already understood that it was time that mattered to the King.

Slowly she took off her bonnet and the gown in which she had arrived and Mithra suggested that she had a rest before dinner.

She found herself thinking of the King as a man and her husband, and she knew that not only was he old, but as a man she found him repellent.

He had not in fact said one pleasant word to her since she had arrived, and had merely been in a hurry to get through everything that appertained to her welcome.

It struck her that he resented being pressured into marriage and just as she had no wish to marry him, he had no wish to marry her.

"Perhaps we will be able to go our separate ways," she told herself as she stared at her reflection in the mirror.

Then she saw the King's thin, rather cruel mouth and what seemed to her to be a hostile expression in his eyes, and she was frightened.

Frightened not only at the idea of him as her husband, but of something else – something she sensed but could not put into words.

Something that was so vividly there that she was terrified.

# CHAPTER FIVE

Giōna looked at herself in the mirror and thought that no one could complain that she did not look attractive for what was to be an important public appearance.

Her mother had chosen for her a pale yellow gown the colour of spring sunshine, which threw into prominence the soft gold of her hair and made her eyes seem more mystical than usual.

The bonnet that went with it was trimmed with king-cups, and she thought as Mithra handed her her gloves and a small satin-bag which matched her gown that even the King must think she looked nice.

Just as she was about to go downstairs there came a knock on the door and when Mithra opened it a flunkey said:

"Before Her Royal Highness joins His Majesty, Sir Edward Bowden would like to speak to her in an Ante-Room, and I'm waiting to escort Her Royal Highness there."

Giōna could hear what was said and she hurried forward saying:

"I am ready."

The flunkey was a middle-aged man who she imagined must have been at the Palace for some years, and she therefore asked him:

"Have you seen many changes while you have been working here?"

She spoke slowly in Slavonian and he paused before he replied:

"I was here when I was a young man, Your Royal Highness, with the last King, and the Palace was a very happy place in those days."

From the way he spoke there was no need for him to say more, and Giōna walked beside him along the passages and down a magnificent double staircase which led to the marble hall.

He took her into what was a small, rather austere room which she guessed was mainly used for people waiting for an audience with the King.

"Good-morning, Your Excellency!" Giōna said. "Are you coming with me this morning to the House of Parliament where I understand His Majesty and I are to receive a magnificent wedding-gift from the members?"

"I shall be accompanying Your Royal Highness," Sir Edward replied, "but first I have something of importance to say to you."

"What is it?" Giōna enquired a little apprehensively.

"Last night I was informed by His Majesty and several of his Advisers that it would be best if you changed your name."

"Changed my name?" Giōna exclaimed in astonishment.

This was something she had certainly not expected.

Sir Edward looked uncomfortable.

"His Majesty thinks it would be more appropriate if as our reigning Queen you had a name that was more usual."

Giōna stared for a moment, then she said:

"I believe what His Majesty is really saying is that my

name is Greek and therefore more likely to be appreciated by the Slavonians than the Austrians."

She spoke sharply and Sir Edward glanced over his shoulder before he said:

"I was afraid Your Royal Highness might be a little upset at his suggestion, but His Majesty is very anxious that you should be married to him by a name with which he is familiar."

Giōna did not speak and Sir Edward went on:

"He has made several suggestions – Matilda, which was the name of his mother, Wilhelmina, for which he says he has always had a fondness, or perhaps Gertrude."

Giōna drew in her breath. Then she said:

"My name was chosen for me by my father and mother when I was christened, and as my father was Greek it is something of which I am very proud. Will you inform His Majesty that I would never think of taking another name which is certainly something my father would not have wished me to do were he alive."

Sir Edward sighed.

"His Majesty will be very – disappointed."

He hesitated before the last word and Giōna knew he was going to say 'displeased'.

She suddenly felt a pride she had not known she possessed, make her determined that she would not be overwhelmed or trodden on by the King, and that the first step he appeared to be taking was to put pressure on her to lose her identity.

"My name is Giōna," she said firmly, "and that is how I shall be married. If the King does not welcome it, I feel the people of Slavonia will."

She knew by the expression on Sir Edward's face that this was the last thing with which the King was concerned.

Because she had no wish to argue any further she turned towards the door saying:

91

"I feel His Majesty will be waiting for me and, as Your Excellency knows, I must not be late!"

Before Sir Edward could speak she walked out into the hall where, as she expected, an *Aide-de-Camp* was waiting to escort them to the King.

When they reached him Giōna curtsied and he said quite genially:

"Good-morning! You are punctual which is a good thing, because we have a great deal to do and the carriage is waiting."

He did not pause for her reply but walked ahead of her back into the hall and out through the front door.

She could not help thinking that, disagreeable though he was, he at least looked magnificent in his uniform blazing with decorations, a blue ribbon across one shoulder, and the same plumed hat he had worn to meet her at the station.

She did not miss the fact that there seemed to be a great number of soldiers lining the route from the Palace to the gates, and there was a troop of Cavalry to ride in front and another behind the carriage in which they were to be conveyed.

She was not however to be alone with the King, for sitting opposite them was an Officer, almost as resplendent as the King himself, and a fat, dumpy German woman whom Giōna had already learned last night was to be one of her two Ladies-in-Waiting.

Of these one was a Baroness and the other a Countess, both grey-haired and nearing or over fifty.

She felt that somebody might have thought it would be more pleasant for her to have at least one of them nearer her own age.

The King made it quite clear that both the Baroness and the Countess would teach her the formalities of Court Life, and Giōna was sure they would be like Governesses, ready to find fault with everything she did.

The Baroness, who was with her now, was obviously terrified of the King, and although Giōna was polite enough to wish her good-morning and say how much she was looking forward to the drive to the House of Parliament, the woman was too nervous to answer her except in monosyllables.

She therefore gave her attention to the crowd through which they were passing who had started cheering as soon as they left the Palace gates.

Again Giōna was aware that the soldiers guarding the route were very close to each other and, what was more, they faced the crowds with their backs to the Royal carriage which meant they were watching for any likely assailant amongst the populace.

However, everybody seemed to be in a happy mood, the sun was shining, the trees were in bloom, and the children, many of whom were seated on their father's shoulders, were waving small paper Union Jacks.

Giōna waved back, aware that once again the King was sitting stiffly at her side, making no effort to acknowledge the cheers.

The horses were drawing them as quickly as they had when they brought her from the station, and after they had passed down one wide avenue and were turning into another, Giōna said to the King:

"Surely it is unnecessary to move so swiftly? These people must have waited a long time to see us, and yet we pass them in a flash."

"We have no time to hang about," the King replied. "Besides, it might be dangerous."

"Do you really think they might throw a bomb or try to shoot at us with so many soldiers lining the route?" Giōna asked.

She spoke lightly, but the King was scowling as he answered:

"There is no point in taking unnecessary risks."

The way he spoke made Giōna turn once again with relief to the people who were cheering them.

They passed into a large, impressive Square and ahead of her she saw the House of Parliament.

It was a finely designed building of grey stone and in front of it was a formal garden with a wide central path carpeted in red, over which she and the King were to walk when they left the carriage.

There were spectators on either side of the path being held back by a barrier of soldiers so tall that Giōna felt it must be impossible for the people to see anything over their shoulders.

She smiled and waved her hand in response to their cheers, aware that the King had, the moment he stepped out of the carriage, set off quickly towards the steps leading into the Parliament building.

She could see the Prime Minister at the top of them waiting with the members of his Cabinet.

Giōna was having difficulty in keeping up with the King when a small child, a little boy of perhaps three years of age, slipped between two of the soldiers watching the crowd and ran towards her.

He had one flower in his hand, a rose, and he was holding it out to her eagerly.

Giōna stopped and an Officer who had been in front of the soldiers came hurrying towards the child intent on moving him away.

Giōna reached him first.

She bent down, crouching a little so that her face was almost on a level with his, as she took the rose from him and said softly in Slavonian:

"Thank you, that is a lovely flower you have brought me."

"For pretty Princess," the child lisped.

She smiled at him and asked:

"What is your name?"

"Your Royal Highness," the Officer said before he could speak, "this child has no right to be here. I must take him away."

Giōna looked up at him smiling.

"Nonsense!" she said. "He has every right to give me a flower and that at least cannot be considered dangerous."

She saw the Officer was not smiling, but looking rather fierce and rising she picked the little boy up in her arms saying:

"I will take him back to his mother."

The Officer gasped but did not know how to interfere.

Giōna carried the child back to where she could see a woman holding out her arms while two soldiers forcibly restrained her from joining her son.

The small boy was quite happy to be carried by Giōna, and when she reached his mother there was a sudden silence as if everybody was too astonished by what was happening to make a sound.

"Your son is a very handsome little boy," Giōna said in Slavonian. "How old is he?"

"Just – t-three years – old – Gracious – Lady," the woman replied, stammering a little as if overcome by being spoken to.

Giōna handed the small boy to her and said:

"I am very pleased with the rose he has brought me. Thank you very much!"

The mother took the child from her, then as she turned to rejoin the King the cheers broke out.

The King, as if he found it impossible to believe what was happening, was standing at the foot of the steps with what she thought was an extremely angry expression on his face.

"I am sorry to keep Your Majesty waiting," Giōna said a little breathlessly.

"That child had no right to be allowed to intrude," the

King replied. "You should have ignored him. The Officer in Charge will be reprimanded for negligence."

"A child as small as that can creep through anywhere," Giōna smiled. "He brought me a rose."

She held it up to show it to him.

"I thought it a very touching gesture."

"It is disgraceful, absolutely disgraceful!" the King exclaimed.

He started to stamp up the steps, each footfall seeming as if it repeated the word until they reached the top.

The Prime Minister greeted them with a long and, Giōna thought, again very boring speech of welcome.

Then she found herself on a platform at one end of the huge hall with all the Members of Parliament and their wives seated in front of them.

They rose when she and the King appeared, clapping politely but not, she thought, with the same enthusiasm as had been shown by the crowd.

After she and the King were seated the speeches began and she thought each one was more pompous than the last.

They were of course all delivered in German and it was not difficult for her to see that the Cabinet were all either Austrians or Germans while she was sure without being told that the majority of the Members of Parliament were Slavonians.

The first part of the proceedings took nearly an hour before the wedding-present, which was a large and resplendent gold table ornament, was at last presented to them.

The King then thanked the assembled company for their generosity and said he hoped that his marriage, which represented an alliance between Slavonia and Great Britain, would bring the country the peace which it so ardently desired.

Only some of the Members of Parliament, Giōna

noticed, applauded, when he referred to her, and she guessed that those who abstained were Slavonians who thought the British were bolstering up a régime of which they did not approve.

There was no question of her being able to say anything, and when the ceremony was over she found it impossible to speak to anyone except the Cabinet, while the Members of Parliament and their wives moved out through another door.

Then once again the King and she were walking back the way they had come, and when they passed the point where the little boy had run out she thought the cheers were louder and more genuine than those she had heard before.

The women were waving their handkerchiefs and the men their hats, and there seemed to be more children sitting on their father's shoulders than there had been previously.

They drove back to the Palace at the same pace as they had come from it, and only when they had left the carriages and were moving up the steps of the Palace itself did the King say:

"Another time ignore anyone who approaches you, whether it is a child, a man, or a woman. I shall contrive to make certain that there is no question of anyone again passing the body-guards. Unfortunately our troops are not as efficient as I would wish them to be, seeing we have to use the natives of this country."

"You mean they are Slavonian?"

"Of course they are Slavonian," the King replied. "Stupid fools without a brain in their head! We have the right men to train them, but they will not always learn."

He spoke angrily, then added:

"If they are ever again so lax as to permit the kind of incident that happened this morning, you will take no notice. Do you understand?"

They had reached the hall by this time and Giōna thought it best not to argue with the King in front of the servants.

At the same time she thought it was a great deal of fuss about one small boy aged three, and she still carried the rose he had given her.

. . . . . . .

Luncheon was once again a long-drawn-out meal and when it was over Giōna retired to what she thought of as her private Sitting-Room, only to find that both her Ladies-in-Waiting came with her.

"I thought, Your Royal Highness," the Baroness said, "that this would be a good opportunity for us to instruct you in some of the etiquette that His Majesty expects here in the Palace."

Giōna shook her head.

"I am sorry," she said, "but what I wish to do now is o be alone to write to my mother. I want to tell her what has happened since I arrived and also to describe the journey."

The Baroness looked worried.

"I hope you will not tell the Princess of the regrettable and outrageous attack made on your train by those terrible revolutionaries. I feel sure it would upset her."

"As far as I can ascertain," Giōna replied, "there were only two of them wounded, and we were all unharmed, so it might have been much worse."

"Your Royal Highness is very brave," the Baroness said, "but I hear His Majesty has given the order that any revolutionary who is caught in the next month will be summarily hanged as a reprisal for their behaviour on your arrival."

"Oh, no!" Giōna cried. "That is cruel and unnecessary, and the man they catch may be entirely innocent."

"All revolutionaries should be exterminated!" the Baroness asserted. "Do you not agree, Countess?"

"I do indeed!" the other Lady-in-Waiting replied. "If His Majesty does not keep them under control we shall none of us be able to sleep in our beds without being afraid."

Giōna decided it would be a mistake to say too much. At the same time she was appalled by the violence of the King's reaction.

She could not imagine a severer punishment could have been devised if, according to the plan 'The Invisible One' had told her, the whole train had been burned with her in it.

She had however made it quite clear that she wished to be alone, and looking as if they expected they would be reprimanded for not doing their duty, the two Ladies-in-Waiting withdrew.

Giōna sat down at the desk in the corner of the room and started to write to her mother and Chloris.

She told them how much she missed them and began her account with her arrival at the Station at Dūric, thinking perhaps the Baroness was right and it would be a mistake to upset her mother by describing the incident on the train.

She had already written them long letters when she was on board ship and made a very amusing story of how sea-sick everybody was.

Also she related how, after all the Ambassador's fuss about her being chaperoned, both he and the Lady Bowden had succumbed to the stormy waves in the Bay of Biscay and had not been seen again until they reached the smoother waters of the Mediterranean.

She now described to her mother how boring the long speeches in German had been both at her arrival and today in the House of Parliament.

She finished:

*"If only you were here, Mama and Chloris, I would*

99

*have somebody to laugh with, but there are very few smiles in the Palace, and I am sure it is because the King has no time for them."*

She had already described how the King hurried over everything and the speed at which they rushed through the streets.

She was just finishing her letter when Mithra came into the room from the bedroom.

"Excuse me, Your Royal Highness," she said, "but a servant has come upstairs to tell you that a deputation of mothers and children have just arrived at the door. The children have all brought you flowers, and the mothers, although they know it is an imposition, ask if it would be possible to speak to you."

Giōna put down her pen.

"Of course," she said. "Have the deputation shown into one of the rooms. I will come down immediately."

Mithra hesitated.

"The servant who brought the message, Your Royal Highness, says that he cannot find the Chief Steward at this time, as he is having a rest, and he is therefore not quite certain what is the right thing to do."

"The right thing to do is to show the women into one of the rooms, as I told you," Giōna replied. "I cannot believe there are many of them."

"About a dozen, I think, Your Royal Highness, and their children."

"Tell the servants to do as I say," Giōna insisted.

Mithra hurried away and Giōna finished her letter, put it into an envelope and addressed it.

Then she went into the bedroom where Mithra was waiting and said:

"Have my letter posted, Mithra, and where is the deputation?"

"They are in the first room on the right as you come in

at the front door, Your Royal Highness," Mithra replied, "although I am not quite certain you are doing the right thing."

"This is the first deputation I have ever received," Giōna answered, "and I am going to enjoy it!"

She laughed as she spoke, then ran impetuously along the corridor and down the stairs, fearing that if she did not hurry somebody might send the deputation away before she could see them.

A servant, and she suspected it was the one who had come upstairs, opened the door for her leading out of the marble hall, and she went into what was apparently a small Ante-Room.

She found, as Mithra had said, a dozen women waiting, each one accompanied by a small child or children, holding posies of flowers.

They were obviously overcome with their surroundings and were standing in a little group looking nervous.

At the same time Giōna appreciated that many of them were extremely good-looking, some of the younger ones really lovely, with enormous eyes and long hair which fell over their shoulders.

They were all in native costume with its pretty velvet bodice, flared skirt and embroidered apron that was almost universal in the Balkans.

As Giōna appeared they made a murmur of delight that was more eloquent than if they had spoken.

"How kind of you to come to see me," Giōna said in Slavonian.

As she spoke they gave a cry of delight and one of them exclaimed, and she knew it was the mother of the little boy she had carried:

"I told you Her Royal Highness speaks our language!"

"I have been learning it all the way here," Giōna said. "But if I make mistakes you must forgive me and tell me what I really ought to have said."

"It is wonderful that we can understand Your Royal Highness, and you can understand us! But we never expected an English Princess to be as beautiful as you, or so clever!"

Giōna laughed.

Then she took the flowers from the children, asking their names and their ages and finding them all very attractive.

In fact, the little girls were, as she had written to her mother, as lovely as angels.

"I had no idea you were all so beautiful in Slavonia!" she said. "But it is only right that such a beautiful country should contain beautiful people!"

"You too are very beautiful, Your Royal Highness," one of the more voluble of the women replied, "and perhaps things will be different now that you have arrived."

"Different? In what way?" Giōna asked.

There was a little pause, then they said:

"No one cares about us. The Schools are bad and there are not enough teachers. Our children, however clever they are, cannot get on and improve themselves."

"That is wrong!" Giōna exclaimed.

"I know, Your Royal Highness, but although some of our Members of Parliament complain over and over again, nothing is done for the real people of the country."

Giōna repressed what she wanted to say, knowing it would be a mistake.

Instead she asked the women about their lives and found, as she expected, that their husbands were all in lowly occupations and there was only one whose husband was a clerk in one of the Government Offices.

She realised too from what they said that they were very poor, and it was not hard to guess that it was those who lived in the City who suffered the most because the people in the country could at least grow their own food.

There was a hundred things she wanted to say, but she knew it would be indiscreet and finally, because she was afraid they might be interrupted, she thought it wise to draw their visit to an end.

"I wish I had something to give the children," she said.

Then on an impulse she rang the bell.

The door was opened instantly which made her think the servants on duty had been listening outside.

"Will you see if you can find some biscuits, cakes or chocolate for the children?" she asked. "I feel sure the Chef can provide something. There are not many of them."

She spoke in German and the servant bowed and disappeared.

"Please, Your Royal Highness, you must not bother about us," one of the women said. "We thought it was very daring of us to come here at all. We have never been inside the Palace before, but after you have been so kind, we wanted to tell you how much we admire you."

"I have enjoyed meeting you," Giōna replied, "and I hope to have the opportunity of talking to many of the people in Slavonia as I have been able to do with you."

She knew by the expressions on their faces that they thought this very unlikely.

Then fortunately, far quicker than she expected, the servant returned with a trayful of fancy pastries with which the children were delighted and so were their mothers.

They ate quickly, then as if they sensed as Giōna did that it would be a mistake for them to linger any longer, they took their leave.

Giōna tried to shake hands with the mothers, but to her embarrassment they curtsied, then went down on their knees to kiss her hand and the children followed their example.

They were so effusive in their gratitude that it was pathetic and when she waved them goodbye from the top of the steps, she thought, if nothing else, she had made a few friends in Dūric.

Then as she turned back to go through the high ornamental door an *Aide-de-Camp* came to her side.

"His Majesty wishes to speak to you, Your Royal Highness."

"Where is he?" Giōna asked.

She was aware that her heart had given a rather frightened jump as if she knew she had been doing something wrong and had been caught out like a naughty schoolgirl.

"His Majesty is in his private Study," the *Aide-de-Camp* replied. "May I show you the way?"

Giōna followed him for what seemed miles along corridors to a part of the Palace where she guessed the King has his private apartments.

The room into which she was shown was large, dark, and somehow so obviously Germanic it might have come straight from the North of Europe, without any alterations being made to it.

The walls were covered with heavy dark panelling, the chairs and sofa did not look very comfortable and were upholstered in brown leather, there was a huge impressive desk piled with papers, and the pictures were quite obviously of the King's ancestors in black carved frames.

The King had discarded most of the decorations which he had worn in the morning, but he was still looking very impressive and he rose from the desk as Giōna entered and stood watching her approach.

As she reached his side and curtsied he said:

"I have been informed that without my permission you have received a number of women and their children who had no right to approach you, and those who admitted them to the Palace must have been insane to do so!"

He sounded so fierce and so angry that instead of feeling frightened Giōna merely wanted to laugh.

"You are taking it far too seriously," she said. "They were just a few young mothers who wanted to see me, and who brought their children with them. I was very touched at their doing so, and I hope that it will form a bond between myself and the Slavonian people which might not have happened if the little boy had not brought me a rose on the way to the House of Parliament this morning."

The King stared at her as if he could hardly believe what he was hearing.

Because he did not speak she walked away from him to stand in front of the rather austere mantelpiece and looked around the room.

"Are these your ancestors?" she asked indicating the pictures. "I hope you will tell me about them."

The King walked from the desk towards her.

"What I am telling you," he said in a voice of thunder, "is that now you are in my country you will behave yourself. How dare you ask the scum of the gutter into my Palace! How dare you entertain them with my food! It is something you will not do again!"

"Why not?" Giōna asked. "I fail to see anything sinister in the fact that a few women should call on their future Queen because they realise that she is fond of children."

"You are arguing with me," the King fumed, "and you must understand that is something I cannot have! How dare you defy me? If you think you can bring your British arrogance and your British contempt for foreigners here, you are very much mistaken!"

He almost spat the words at her.

Then when she involuntarily looked away from him embarrassed by the fury she saw in his face, he suddenly raised his hand and struck her violently across the cheek saying:

"Listen to me, curse you! I will have no British defiance or British superiority in my Palace, and the sooner you learn that the better!"

Half stunned by the blow, Giōna only just had time to look at him in sheer astonishment before he seized her by her shoulders and began to shake her.

He was a large, strong man, and he shook her violently as a terrier might shake a rabbit until the pins fell from her head and her hair was shaken down over her shoulders.

He went on shaking her, rocking her backwards and forwards so roughly that the breath was squeezed from her body and she could not even see him, let alone beg him to stop.

Then suddenly, before she could make a sound of fear, he flung her down onto the leather sofa so that she hit her head against the hard cushion.

"That will teach you to do as you are told!" he roared. "And the next time you disobey my orders I will beat you until you learn the folly of doing so!"

He paused for breath before he went on, working himself up into a rage that seemed almost to make him foam at the mouth.

"I have no intention of being defied by my wife because she comes from a country which tries to impose its will upon the whole of Europe! I am not afraid of your Queen, omnipotent though she may think she is, and I will make sure you do not argue, let alone disobey me, by whipping you as all revolutionaries, whoever they may be, should be whipped!"

He looked down at her and Giōna thought with a sudden stab of fear that he was going to hit her again.

Instead she realised as he did not go on speaking that suddenly a different expression had come into his eyes.

They had narrowed, and she thought as his lips parted and he was still silent that there was something sinister and horrifying about him that had not been there before.

Then his hand reached out and he pulled at the soft silk at the base of her neck and with a rough gesture which took her by surprise, tore it open to her breasts and she gave a scream of horror.

Her hands went up as if to protect herself, as she realised instinctively that what he was about to do was even more horrible than the way he had struck her.

Just as he started to bend forwards towards her the door opened and one of the senior Equerries came into the room.

The King who was still holding onto the torn silk at her neck, looked up.

"What do you want?" he asked angrily.

"Something very important has occurred, Your Majesty, which requires your presence immediately in the Throne Room."

The King hesitated.

"It cannot wait?"

"No, Your Majesty."

Reluctantly the King's fingers let go of the torn silk of Giōna's gown.

Then walking almost like a man in his sleep, he turned towards the door with the Equerry close beside him.

As they left the room Giōna felt everything go dark and thought she was about to faint.

Then because she was terrified that the King might return, she forced herself to rise from the sofa on shaking legs, and holding onto the furniture she gradually reached the door.

Before she opened it she drew a deep breath, still feeling as if she might subside into the darkness that seemed about to engulf her.

Then knowing that somehow she must escape she

pulled at the door and thought for one terrified moment that she had been locked in, but at last it opened.

Holding onto the torn silk of her gown she bent her head and hurried along the passage hoping she could find her way back to her room without going through the main hallway.

She found a secondary staircase which took her up to the first floor.

Then at last, feeling so limp and bewildered that she kept bumping into pieces of furniture, she found a corridor she recognised and knew that at the end of it was her own bedroom.

She opened the door, heard Mithra give a little cry of horror at the sight of her, and collapsed in her arms.

She must have been unconscious because when she could think again Mithra had somehow lifted her onto the bed and was holding a glass of water to her lips.

"Drink a little, Your Royal Highness," she begged. "Please, drink a little."

Giōna did as she was told and shut her eyes to drift away into a grey world where vaguely, far away, she could hear Mithra asking somebody to bring her some brandy.

Then she knew her shoes were being removed from her feet and her gown loosened before what must have been quite a long time later Mithra was holding a glass to her lips again, but this time it contained brandy.

Giōna wanted to refuse, but Mithra insisted, and after she had drunk a few sips she felt the fiery liquid running down into her body and the darkness vanished.

She would have sat up in bed, but Mithra said:

"No, rest, Your Royal Highness. You have had a shock."

Giōna however remained sitting up.

"I . . I have to . . go away," she said. "I cannot . . stay here!"

"He will not let you go, Your Royal Highness."

"H . how can I .. stay?" Giōna asked frantically. "He .. struck .. me!"

She remembered as she spoke that he had not only shaken her but had threatened to whip her.

Worse, she could see his face as in a nightmare, his eyes narrowing, his lips parting as he reached out to tear at her gown.

She gave a cry like that of a child frightened beyond endurance and held onto Mithra.

"Help me to .. get away .. help me .. Mithra!"

"It is impossible, Your Royal Highness, you must understand. You are to be married tomorrow. If you escape from the Palace they will never let you leave the country."

"I .. I cannot stay here .. with him .. he is cruel .. bestial .. horrible!"

"I know, Your Royal Highness. I know!"

Giōna was still.

"You know? What do you know?"

"What he is like, Your Royal Highness."

"You mean .. he assaults people .. beats them?"

"Not people, Your Royal Highness, but very young girls. They are brought to him here in the Palace, which is wicked, criminal, but what can we do?"

Giōna fell back against the pillows, her eyes wide.

Now she understood what had been kept secret from her, what the two men speaking in German on the battleship had meant when she overheard them say that she was too young to cope with him and the English did not like that sort of thing.

She felt the horror of it sweep over her until she knew that rather than endure such degradation and humiliation she would rather die.

In fact, that was what she would have to do.

Then as she looked at Mithra's anxious face, frightened

by her silence, she remembered a quiet, deep voice saying:

"If you find it unbearable I will try to save you."

Quite suddenly she knew what she could do.

It *was* unbearable and there was only one person in the whole country who could save her.

She was silent for several minutes as she tried to think and felt Mithra pressing a compress of cold water to the burning mark on her cheek where the King had struck her.

"If he does not save me," she told herself, "then I must die!"

Now she had the terrifying knowledge that there was very little time before the marriage tomorrow, and she pushed Mithra's hand to one side and got out of bed.

"You should not move, Your Royal Highness," Mithra said in a worried voice. "Please, rest!"

"There is something I have to do!" Giōna replied.

She walked unsteadily to the desk where she had written the letter to her mother.

Drawing a piece of writing-paper from the leather holder, she tore it in half, then in half again.

Then in very small writing she wrote the same words in English that 'The Invisible One' had used to her:

*"Help me – For God's sake – help me!"*

# CHAPTER SIX

"I have failed," Giōna said to herself, "and there is nothing more I can do."

She felt Mithra arranging her hair, then having placed a beautiful lace veil which her mother had given her to bring from England over her head, she put on the top of it a tiara of stars which Giōna learnt had been amongst the Slavonian Crown Jewels for many centuries.

She had been told that she would wear this to the Cathedral, where it would be removed when the King placed a crown on her head, and afterwards she would wear it for the return journey.

She hardly listened to what was being said in a monotonous tone by one of her Ladies-in-Waiting because she was quite certain that she would never reach the Cathedral and certainly not go through the ceremony of marriage with the King.

She could not bear to think of him without shuddering.

Her cheek was still sore from where he had struck her, while both her shoulders ached from the violence with which he had dug his nails into her soft skin as he shook her.

When she wrote her cry for help to 'The Invisible One', she had felt as if she vibrated towards him as she had when they had sat opposite each other in the darkness of the railway carriage.

Then rising to her feet she said to Mithra who was watching her anxiously:

"Can I trust you?"

The woman's eyes widened, then she replied:

"I love Your Royal Highness, and I would do anything to help you."

"What I want you to do," Giōna said, "is to find Captain Darius. Make quite certain he is alone and give him this piece of paper. Ask him to take it immediately to 'The Invisible One'."

She saw Mithra stiffen as she spoke and her eyes looked up at her wildly.

Then after a second's astonishment she took the piece of paper from Giōna's hands and said:

"I'll not fail Your Royal Highness. Please rest while I'm gone."

"I will try to," Giōna said and went back to the bed.

She lay with her eyes shut praying that by some miracle 'The Invisible One' would save her from being married to a man whose behaviour was so terrifying that she could not bear to think of it.

She must have dozed a little, for it was quite a long time before Mithra returned. Then she said in a low voice as if she was frightened:

"I found Captain Darius, Your Royal Highness, and he understood."

Giōna then allowed Mithra to undress her and she got into bed.

A little later she told Mithra to inform one of her Ladies-in-Waiting that she would not be coming down to dinner.

The Baroness came hurrying to her bedroom.

"Your maid tells me that Your Royal Highness is not well," she said. "But it is impossible for you not to dine with His Majesty this evening. Several of his relations will be present as well as Sir Edward and Lady Bowden."

Giōna did not answer and after a moment she went on:

"I feel sure His Majesty will wish to talk to you, to give you his last minute instructions about the ceremony tomorrow, and he will be extremely perturbed if you are not present."

"His Majesty will understand that I am indisposed," Giōna said in a hard voice and after that refused to discuss it any further.

The Baroness was obviously upset and bewildered that Giōna had changed from being so charming and amenable without there being any apparent reason for it.

"I will see no one else, Mithra!" Giōna said.

When the maid brought her some supper she found it difficult to eat anything.

When she was alone again she lay awake, praying that Captain Darius would somehow get in touch with 'The Invisible One' and that he would keep his promise.

Yet she knew how heavily the Palace was guarded, and she could think of no way by which he could enter it without being apprehended by the sentries who were posted at every entrance or could evade the soldiers who were permanently patrolling the grounds.

"I am determined to get away whatever happens," Giōna told herself, and wondered if it would be possible for her to creep out of the Palace and meet 'The Invisible One' outside.

She had hoped that Captain Darius would send her a message of some sort by Mithra.

But her maid had said goodnight without giving her one, and the moment she was alone all the seemingly insurmountable difficulties of her situation swept over her.

And yet at the end of a very long dark tunnel she

persuaded herself she could still see a glimmer of light and hope.

Now however she knew she had failed and it was too late.

Already her two Ladies-in-Waiting, fussing like a couple of old hens, had gone ahead of her to the Cathedral, and she knew that in a few minutes she would have to go downstairs to where Sir Edward would be waiting to escort her there.

Outside the front door there would be a closed carriage in which she was to drive with him to the Cathedral with a troop of Cavalry leading the way and another troop behind.

The King would have already left and she was trapped as surely as any wild animal so that there was no escape.

Once again she told herself the only thing she could do once she was married would be somehow to die before the King touched her.

It was impossible to think of him without seeing the expression on his face when he had torn her gown, and now she knew that even though she was his wife she would have to endure the same fate as the young girls who were brought to the Palace for his amusement.

Perhaps her ordeal would be even worse because she knew from what he had said when he raged at her that he loathed the British.

He would want to hurt her not only because she defied him but because she stood for everything that he hated and resented about her country.

"I must die," Gióna said and without meaning to, said the words aloud.

"What did Your Royal Highness say?" Mithra asked as she finished setting the tiara in place.

There was another veil to put over Gióna's face which could be removed after the ceremony without upsetting the arrangement of the veil which covered her head.

Mithra picked it up and as she did so said again: "I didn't hear what Your Royal Highness said," there was a knock on the door.

Giōna felt sure that this was to tell her that Sir Edward was waiting and she closed her eyes with the agony of it, wondering what would happen if she refused to leave for the Cathedral but feeling that if she did so she would be taken there forcibly.

Then as she heard Mithra give a little murmur of surprise she turned her head and saw that the door of her room had opened. It was not a footman who stood there, but Captain Darius.

He put out his hand towards her and said in a low voice:

"We have five seconds – come!"

Quite suddenly Giōna felt the dark depression that had enveloped her like a cloud, lift and she sprang to her feet.

Without speaking Mithra picked up her train and threw it over her arm.

Then as Giōna ran towards Captain Darius to take his hand, he said to Mithra:

"Delay letting them know Her Royal Highness has gone for as long as you possibly can. Then collect anything you think she will need and follow us."

Giōna had the impression that Mithra's eyes lit up, then Captain Darius was drawing her down the passage and they were moving so quickly that she was afraid of stumbling.

Still holding her hand he led her to the far end of the corridor opposite to that which led to the main hall, and hurried her down a side staircase.

At the bottom of it there was a small door that led out into an ancient courtyard where from the scaffolding erected there it looked as if it was in the process of being repaired.

There was a closed carriage drawn by four horses, and

the moment Captain Darius lifted Giōna into it, the horses drove off.

As Giōna sat down on the padded seat she realised there were blinds drawn over the windows so that no one could look in and they were in darkness.

She knew that they passed through the gate leading out of the Palace gardens because there was the sound of the sentries coming to attention.

With a hint of amusement in his voice Captain Darius spoke for the first time.

"They believe someone had died in the Palace," he said, "and in case the death would spoil the festive spirit of the wedding-guests we are removing the corpse to a more appropriate place."

Giōna could not help laughing at this ingenious piece of deception and in the darkness of the carriage she felt as if she had suddenly stepped into the sunlight.

As the horses galloped on, now working up a terrific speed, she asked:

"How did you do it? I was in despair before you came and thought I should have to marry the King."

"It was not easy to arrange everything so quickly," Captain Darius replied. "We are not out of the wood yet, Princess, and I am afraid there is a hard ride ahead of you."

"A ride?" Giōna enquired.

Captain Darius pulled up the blinds that had covered the windows and now she could see they were already well away from the City and out in the open country and ahead of them were the high, towering mountains.

There was no need for her to say anything. She knew that was where 'The Invisible One' would be, not only out of reach of his enemies, but also with a commanding view of the valley so that it would be impossible for anybody to take him by surprise.

"I thought that as there would be no time for you to

change," Captain Darius said, "you would have to pin up your train. So I have brought you some safety pins."

He held them out in his hand as he spoke, and because it seemed absurdly incongruous and she was so relieved to have escaped from the Palace, Giōna burst out laughing and he laughed too.

It was quite difficult to pin up her train in the swaying carriage, but she managed it.

Then Captain Darius produced a dark scarf for her to wear over her head and a long, light cloak which she knew was worn by Cavalry Officers.

Because of the speed at which they were travelling they did not speak very much, and Giōna deliberately did not ask him more details about what was happening.

She was simply and profoundly grateful for the fact that she had escaped from the Palace, where by now there was doubtless a hue and cry as to what had happened to her.

"Perhaps they will think I am hiding somewhere in the Palace, with its vast number of rooms," she told herself. "In which case it will take a long time for them to look for me."

She could imagine the fury of the King at being kept waiting and she was sure he would viciously punish everybody concerned with looking after her for their negligence.

She was glad therefore that Captain Darius had said that Mithra could follow them.

The horses came to a standstill and still without giving any explanation Captain Darius jumped out and helped her to alight.

She saw that they had reached the foot of the mountains, and awaiting their arrival were four horsemen all mounted on small but sturdy horses which she was sure were used in mountain work and were not only sure-footed but capable of long periods of endurance.

There was one horse with a side-saddle which she knew was for herself, but there was not one for Captain Darius.

She turned to him questioningly saying:

"You are not coming with me?"

He smiled before he replied:

"You will be quite safe, Your Royal Highness, with these gentlemen. I have more work to do in the City before I can join you."

As he finished speaking he bent his head and kissed her hand. Then he lifted her onto the saddle, arranging her skirt with its rather unwieldy pinned-up train so that it was concealed by the Cavalry cloak.

Immediately two of the horsemen rode ahead and as Giōna followed them the other two rode behind her.

She was aware as they moved away that Captain Darius had got back into the carriage and already it was moving back at a tremendous pace towards Dūric.

She wondered curiously exactly what was happening, but was content for the moment to be free and busy seeing that her horse did not stumble over the rough ground as they rose higher and higher up the mountainside.

They rode in silence until after over half-an-hour they moved onto what seemed to be almost a level plateau below the peak of the mountain and for the first time she had sight of other men.

They ran ahead when they saw her approaching, and she was sure they had been waiting for her arrival.

Then the plateau widened out and she saw at the end of it there were a large number of natural caves in the mountainside and on the other side she could see a valley not unlike the one she had just left, except that there were no houses.

To her surprise there were a number of men and women moving about, and she thought there were also some guns, although she could not be certain.

They rode across the level ground, until she saw waiting for her in the entrance of one of the caves one man standing alone.

She had never actually seen him before and had no idea what he looked like, but at her first glance it was as if his vibrations she had felt so strongly in the railway carriage leapt out towards hers, and she knew without being told that here was 'The Invisible One'.

As the horses came to a standstill he moved to Giōna's side and lifting her down from the saddle said:

"You are all right? The journey has not been too much for you?"

She might have expected him to be concerned for her, but she gave a little laugh as she replied:

"Every second was one of sheer delight, simply because I had escaped from the Palace!"

She looked up at him, her eyes very large in her small face as she asked:

"How did you do it? How could you be so wonderful as to spirit me away at the last moment when I thought all was lost?"

"You are not lost," he said in his deep voice, "you are here. And now, if you will come into my somewhat austere lodging place, I want to talk to you."

Giōna turned to smile at the four horsemen who had brought her up the mountain.

"Thank you," she said. "Thank you very much."

Then she followed 'The Invisible One' into his cave and found it very different from what she expected.

To begin with it was large and very high, as high as any of the rooms in the Palace.

There were rugs on the floor and a desk which she recognised as like those which were used in the Army by commanding officers and could be carried on the back of a horse or a mule.

There were also several chairs and she was about to sit

down when she realised that the man beside her was waiting to take her cloak from her.

She unfastened it at the neck, thinking that, although it had been cool climbing the mountain, the sun was now hot and the cloak was really unnecessary.

She also undid the dark scarf that she had put over her head, and untied her hair which she felt must have been disarranged. As she did so 'The Invisible One' said quietly:

"You look very lovely, just as I thought you would be!"

Giōna felt herself blush, then as she looked at him she knew he too was exactly as she might have expected.

There was no doubt that his features were Greek and in fact they reminded her vaguely of her father's face.

His eyes were dark and so was his hair, and he was, as she had seen him silhouetted against the light when he had gone into her bedroom in the train, tall, broad-shouldered with a slender body and narrow hips and the long legs of an athlete.

He was wearing the simple uniform of an ordinary Slavonian soldier, but she knew he had no need of insignia or epaulettes for it to be obvious that he was a commander, a leader of men.

They stood looking at each other as if it was impossible not to do so until, because she felt shy, Giōna looked away and sat down on one of the chairs.

'The Invisible One' sat down in one opposite her, just as he had done in the train, and said:

"First I think you should have something to drink because I am sure you are thirsty. Then we can talk."

As he spoke a man came into the cave bringing a bottle of golden wine and two glasses.

There was a plate of sweetmeats which Giōna recognised from what her father had described to her as favourites in Balkan countries because they were made with nuts and honey.

She sipped her drink and realised that she was in fact, very thirsty, but too excited to be hungry.

The plate of sweetmeats were put on the desk beside her and when the man had left the cave 'The Invisible One' said:

"I managed to do as you asked me to do, Princess, and save you from a marriage which would have been a crime against God and against man. Now I have a suggestion to make which I can only pray will not frighten you."

"Frighten me?" Giōna asked in surprise.

"You are very young," 'The Invisible One' said quietly, "and you should not be involved in the political disturbances of a foreign country. But you are here, and I think you will understand what I am going to ask you to do."

"You *are* frightening me!" Giōna complained.

"I have no wish to do that."

"But you have saved me from marrying a man who I can only think of as insane."

As she spoke 'The Invisible One' could see the shock in her eyes, and as he looked at her he could see the mark on her cheek that was still crimson against the whiteness of her skin.

"What happened?" he asked. "Who has struck you?"

Now there was a note of anger in his voice that had not been there before, and instinctively Giōna put her hand up to her face before she said:

"I cannot speak of it! It was horrible, beastly, obscene, and if you had not brought me away I was determined to kill myself!"

'The Invisible One' drew in his breath, then he bent forward to take Giōna's hand in his.

"Forgive me," he said, "I should have saved you immediately after we talked together in the railway-carriage. I knew then that you were far too young, innocent and sensitive to be involved with a brute like the King, but at that moment I could not see what I could do about it."

"No, of course not," Giōna answered. "But I never knew, I never dreamt, there were men .. like him in the .. world, or that they could .. behave in such an .. outrageous .. manner."

Her voice was very young and lost and she felt 'The Invisible One's' fingers tighten on hers before he said:

"Because of what you have been through, I am afraid to suggest what is in my mind. But will you listen to me, and try not to be afraid?"

"Of course I will listen," Giōna said.

Then as she looked up at him she gave a little cry of horror and said:

"You are not thinking of sending me back .. you would not want me to .. face him again?"

"No, no, of course not!" the man facing her replied. "Do you really think I could subject you again to such torture, both mental and physical, such as you have endured already?"

Giōna gave a little sigh of relief.

"Then nothing you can ask me to do could be as bad as that," she said with a tremulous smile.

"Drink a little wine," 'The Invisible One' said, "then I will tell you what I have in mind."

She obeyed him, feeling the golden wine like sunshine seeping into her body, dispersing the fear that still lingered in her breast.

Then she said:

"First can we start by your telling me your name? I only know you as 'The Invisible One' and now you are no longer invisible!"

He laughed and it was a spontaneous, happy sound.

"My name is Miklōs," he said, "and as I think you already know, I am the son of King Alexandrōs who was the last Slavonian King of this country, and therefore by heredity I have every right to the throne."

"Of course you have," Giōna agreed. "I like the name Miklōs which in England would be Michael, and I think only the Archangel Michael could have spirited me out of the heavily guarded Palace."

"Now you are here and safe from the King," Prince Miklōs said. "But you are still in Slavonia, a country deeply divided within itself."

The way he spoke made Giōna realise that this concerned her.

He released her as he spoke, and she grasped both her hands together and put them in her lap as she raised her eyes to his like a child waiting to be instructed.

"What I have to say to you," he said, "may come as a shock, but it is very, very important for me and for my country."

"I am listening," Giōna replied softly.

"It was, as I think you know, on the insistence of the House of Parliament, but against the personal wishes of the King, that the deputation was sent to England to ask for the help of Britain and, as a token, one of Queen Victoria's relatives, to preserve our independence."

"I am sure now that the King himself had no wish for a British bride," Giōna said remembering the fury with which he had raged at her for being British.

"That is true," Prince Miklōs agreed. "He would have been quite happy for Slavonia to become part of the Austrian Empire, but was too afraid of the opposing elements in the country to admit it."

He paused as if he was thinking deeply and Giōna waited, wondering what he had to tell her.

"Queen Victoria's reply to the Slavonian request for help was exactly what we had hoped for," Prince Miklōs went on. "She sent one of her relatives to sit upon the throne and thus make it quite clear to the Austrians and anybody else with designs on this country that it was under the protection of the Union Jack."

Giōna nodded.

She was aware of all this and she could not quite see what Prince Miklōs was leading up to. Then he said:

"I cannot believe that the Queen had any idea of the depths of depravity to which King Ferdinand has sunk. But for the sake of Slavonia I am asking you still to do what was intended when you came very bravely and alone to this country to save it."

"I .. I do not .. understand."

Prince Miklōs smiled.

"I am putting it very badly," he said, "but quite simply what I am asking you is to marry the King and make sure that in the future Slavonia is safe."

Giōna stared at him in horror, as if she could not believe what he had said.

Then once again he reached out and took her hand in his and said:

"Not King Ferdinand, who would never have become King but for the stupidity of the Statesmen when my father died, but the rightful King, the King who is a Slavonian and whom the majority of the people love, as they will love you."

Giōna stared at him again. Then she said in a voice he could hardly hear:

"Are .. you suggesting .. that I .. m . marry you?"

"I am not suggesting it," he replied, "I am begging you, if necessary on my knees to do so."

His hand tightened over hers as he said:

"I swear I will try to make you happy, and I believe that, when we get to know each other, we shall have many things in common."

He paused for a moment to look down into her eyes, wide and a little frightened and astonished by what he was saying.

Then he asked very softly:

"Will you marry me, my brave little Princess? You saved my life, and now I am asking you to save my throne."

"Is that what you .. really want?" Giōna asked, so surprised that she was not quite certain what she was saying.

"I know it is a great deal to ask of you after all you have been through," Prince Miklōs replied. "But looking at it from an entirely practical point of view, I know that if I am married to a wife sent from England by Queen Victoria to ensure the independence of this country, the whole populace, even those who are timid and afraid of the Austrians, will rally to me.

"What is more," he went on, "I am sure that the rank and file in the Army under Austrian and German Officers will mutiny against them and then there will be nothing King Ferdinand can do but abdicate."

Giōna drew in her breath.

"If you really .. think that will .. happen," she said, "then of course I must .. marry you."

There was a look both of excitement and joy in the Prince's eyes before he lifted her hand and for the second time she felt his lips on the softness of her skin.

It gave her a strange feeling that she had never known before, and suddenly she felt shy, finding it impossible to look at him.

"Thank you, Princess," he said in a low voice. "I feel I have been cruel to ask so much of you so quickly when you have already been through more than most women could endure. But it is an urgent question of time, for by now everybody of any importance in the country has gathered together in Dūric.

"As this is the moment when you have publicly repudiated King Ferdinand and the Austrian and German faction, and have chosen instead to ally yourself with the

Slavonian Pretender to the throne, the impact will be tremendous!"

He paused then continued:

"Unless I am very much mistaken, the only dissidents will be those who know they will have to clear out of the country and stay out!"

There was a hard note in his voice as he spoke, and Giōna knew how much he must have resented the behaviour of the King and the Austrians and Germans he had placed in positions of power.

"What do you .. want me to do?" Giōna asked.

The Prince smiled, then he replied:

"I want you to rest comfortably in a cave that has been prepared for you until I have made all the arrangements for our wedding which will take place this evening just before dark. Tomorrow, unless you are too afraid, I am going to ask you to be very brave and drive with me to the Capital, where I will claim my rightful place as King of Slavonia."

Giōna looked at him in astonishment. Then she said:

"Surely it will be .. dangerous? Supposing .. somebody throws a .. bomb at you, or tries to .. shoot you?"

"They will not throw a bomb," the Prince said, "because they will be too afraid. If there is any will to resist left amongst the King's guard, they will not wish to kill you, but I must risk being shot by a sniper."

"You would do that?" Giōna cried. "But .. supposing .. just supposing you were .. killed? King Ferdinand might then insist on .. marrying me .. after all!"

There was so much terror in her voice that Prince Miklōs knelt beside her chair and took both her hands in his.

"Listen, Giōna," he said for the first time calling her by her christian name.

"I am listening."

"I swear to you that whatever happens, if you will do as I ask, I will ensure that you are protected, and never will you be asked to marry King Ferdinand, or any man like him. Will you trust me?"

Giōna found as she looked into his eyes, because his face was very near to hers and she was acutely conscious of the closeness of him, that it was impossible to look away.

"I . . trust . . you," she said after a long moment.

He kissed both her hands then rose to his feet.

"Now that is settled," he said, "and I think you have been through enough. I have a feeling that you did not sleep very well last night."

"How could I do . . so?"

"You will sleep now. Some food has been prepared for you, and I have a woman in the camp who will look after you until Mithra arrives."

"You have thought of everything!" Giōna said feeling glad that Mithra would be with her.

"I try to," the Prince replied, "but you will forgive me if you are a little uncomfortable until we are back in the Palace which belonged to my father and four generations of my family before him."

As he spoke he led Giōna from the large cave in which they had been sitting to a smaller one beside it.

It was sparsely furnished, but there was a rug on the floor, a divan which looked comfortable, a table with a mirror on it, and waiting was a middle-aged woman with a kindly face who curtsied as they appeared.

"This is Maria," the Prince said, "she has been with me since I was a boy and spoils me abominably! Is that not true, Maria?"

"Everyone loves Your Royal Highness," Maria smiled, "just as they'll love the beautiful Princess you've brought us."

She said kind and flattering things to Giōna all the time she was helping her out of her wedding-gown and into a loose kimono in which she could rest.

Giōna was so tired, and perhaps too the food and the glass of golden wine helped, that she fell asleep almost as soon as her head touched the pillow.

When she awoke it was to find Mithra was in the cave and her own brushes and combs were set on the table in front of the mirror.

"Mithra! You are here!" she cried happily.

"I'm here, Your Royal Highness, and very, very happy for you!"

She drew in her breath before she went on:

"Now you will marry the real King, a man who is noble and fine and whom we all love and admire."

"You have been told that I am to be married this evening?" Giōna asked.

"It made me very happy, Your Royal Highness."

Giōna sat up on the soft bed.

"What happened after I left?"

"First one footman after another arrived telling you to hurry as Sir Edward was waiting. Then as I packed all the things I thought you might need Sir Edward came himself. He knocked on the door and when I opened it he asked:

"'What is happening? Her Royal Highness is already ten minutes late. The King will be very displeased!'

"I looked surprised and I said:

"'But Her Royal Highness left here a long time ago, Sir. Is she not with you?'

"Sir Edward looked round the bedroom as if he could not believe what I had said. Then he shouted to the footmen and every Equerry who was in the hall to look for you.

"I could see them all rushing about the Palace looking into every room as I slipped down the stairs, as Captain Darius had told me to do, to where a carriage was waiting outside."

"I am so relieved that Prince Miklōs was able to get

you away," Giōna said. "I was afraid you might be punished if I had disappeared."

"I certainly would have been," Mithra said darkly. "I feel sorry for the people in the Palace when the King realises what has happened."

"He will have to make some explanation to the congregation in the Cathedral before that," Giōna said.

Realising that Mithra had no more to tell her she got up, washed and allowed the maid to help her once again into her wedding-gown.

Now for the first time she appreciated how beautiful it was and how grateful she was to Queen Victoria for her present which she knew became her.

Once again Mithra arranged her hair, put on the veil and the tiara which Giōna was told had been worn by Prince Miklōs's mother and grandmother at their weddings.

Then as the sun was sinking crimson and brilliant behind the mountains Prince Miklōs came to the opening of the cave.

He was dressed very differently from the way he had been before, wearing now a uniform which Giōna guessed was that of a Commander in Chief of the Army.

There was as many decorations on his breast as King Ferdinand had worn on his, but he was bare-headed and she thought as he stood with his back to the sunshine that the light that came from him was not of this earth.

It seemed rather to come from some divine power which he exuded because of his vitality, his strength and his nobility.

He came into the cave and asked in a gentle voice:

"You are rested?"

"I slept," Giōna replied.

"I am glad. You are no longer afraid?"

She shook her head.

"Only a little . . shy."

"I find that very attractive."

She looked at him in surprise, then realised that Mithra was there listening to them.

Then he held out his arm.

"Come!" he said smiling. "Our people are waiting for us."

With her hand on his arm they went out of the cave together, and now looking down into the valley of which she had had a glimpse when she arrived, she saw a blaze of light and realised it came from flares.

To her surprise the whole valley seemed to be packed with people.

As they walked slowly down the rough road towards them, Giōna saw that in the centre of an enclosure below them there was an altar on which stood a cross and a great number of candles.

Standing in front of it was a Priest with a long grey beard wearing the hat and elaborate vestments which she recognised as being the mark of the Greek Orthodox Church.

As if he knew what she was thinking Prince Miklōs said:

"I knew that as your father's daughter you would not object to being married by a Greek Priest in the Greek Religion. Nearly all the Slavonians in this part of the country are of Greek origin, and it is the way that I myself worship."

Giōna glanced at him, then she said simply:

"I know my father would be very glad."

They reached the level ground and now it was easier walking over the soft grass.

As they passed through the crowd towards the altar Giōna saw a number of men wearing the uniform of the Slavonian Army and knew that, as the Prince had expected, they had already deserted their Austrian masters.

The rest of the congregation were wearing their national dress, the women with flowers in their hair, the men with buttonholes, and the children scattered flower-petals in front of them as they walked.

The wedding ceremony was then conducted by the Priest and it was a Service so sincere that he made every word he spoke seem beautiful, as if it came from God Himself.

Then the whole valley sang in unison, their voices echoing up towards the sky that was now filling with stars, and it was so moving that Giōna felt the tears come into her eyes.

As if he knew what she was feeling the Prince pressed her hand and she knew he was as deeply moved as she was.

Then as the Service finished everybody started cheering, and their cheers seemed to echo and re-echo amongst the mountains until the whole valley was deafened by them.

"Now," the Prince said as if he was free of the solemnity at last, "we start our wedding-feast, and I hope, Giōna, you are hungry, because I am!"

"Tell me more about what you have been doing," she asked as they sat down at a table which had been prepared for them.

On it there were not only a number of candles but also some very fine goblets set with precious stones which she was sure must have belonged to the Prince's ancestors.

He had no doubt carried them with him when he had gone into exile as 'The Invisible One' to fight secretly against the Austrian régime.

"I have been planning," he said, "and I have been sending messengers down into the City to tell everybody where you were and that we were to be married this evening."

He glanced around him at the soldiers who Giōna

thought had increased quite a lot in numbers since the ceremony started and added:

"As I expected the Army is in disarray, and without the soldiers to support them King Ferdinand and his Austrian Officers will not be able to make much of a stand against us."

By the end of the evening Giōna was certain this was true.

All the time she could see more and more people arriving from the City and realised it must have been a long and arduous walk.

It was obviously because of their strong feelings of patriotism and loyalty to their Prince that they had undertaken it so late at night.

The Prince's people made them welcome with a generous supply of great barrels of beer and kegs of wine, and her health and the Prince's were toasted again and again.

The Prince acknowledged every toast, making each time some appropriate and amusing remark as he did so.

Although she was almost too happy to eat, Giōna appreciated the blue trout caught in one of the silver streams in the mountains, the partridges which were indigenous to the country, and the delicious fruit, some of which she had never tasted before.

There was also golden wine which the Prince told her came from the vineyards of Slavonia and had been planted first by his great-grandfather, the grapes of which had improved year by year.

"We would be very foolish not to export it," he said, "and I feel sure that here is one means by which we can improve the finances of the country, besides a great number of other enterprises which I have in mind."

Giōna was certain that in everything he undertook he would be successful.

When the dancing started he said quietly:

"Now I am going to send you to bed. You have had a very long and exhausting day, and tomorrow will also be very tiring."

Giōna wanted to stay, and yet at the same time she knew he was right.

Because of what she had suffered at the hands of the King, because she had been so afraid, because she had lain awake the night before, terrified that Captain Darius would not be able to find 'The Invisible One' and she would be forced to marry the King, she was indeed very tired.

She felt fatigue sweeping over her like a tidal wave, and it was more and more difficult to keep her eyes open.

The Prince half carried her up the steep path back to the caves, and just before he reached the one in which Mithra was waiting he stopped and said:

"Listen Giōna, there is something important I wish to say to you."

She looked up at him and could see his face very clearly by the light of the moon which was just rising over the highest peaks of the mountains.

"What is it?" she asked a little nervously.

"Do not be afraid," he said. "It is just that you have been brave and generous enough to marry me before we have got to know each other, before we have had the chance to become friends. That is why I am going to suggest that from now on we explore first the possibility of friendship and companionship before I speak to you of love."

Giōna's eyes fell before his and she blushed.

"You are very young," he said softly, "and very, very beautiful. It would be easy for me to say a great many things that tremble on my lips, but I feel somehow you might not believe them. I am therefore going to wait, my little Princess, until the right moment, and I think, because

133

we are very closely attuned to each other, that we shall both be aware when that moment comes."

Once again he pressed her hand to his lips and she found it difficult to know what to say.

This time he turned it over and kissed her palm.

It was something that had never happened to her before, and as she felt the warm insistence of his lips she felt something like a streak of lightning run through her body.

Then before she could understand it, he had released her and taking her into the cave handed her over to Mithra.

"Goodnight, my Princess," he said as he walked away. "Sleep well and God bless you, for today you have saved my country and set it on its way towards happiness and prosperity!"

With that he moved away while Giōna was wishing he would stay longer with her.

# CHAPTER SEVEN

Giōna woke with a sense of excitement and realised that this was a vitally important day, not only in Miklōs's life, but also in hers.

At the same time she knew there were dangers, and despite the feeling of elation she was also aware that deep inside her was a fluttering fear that at the last moment when victory seemed within his grasp he might be killed.

She would have been foolish if she had under-estimated the fury of the King when he learnt what was happening, and she was quite certain that his political advisers no less than the Austrian and German Officers in the Army would want one thing above all – the death of Miklōs.

"Save him, God, please, save him!" she prayed as Mithra dressed her.

She was so intent on her prayers that it was only when she was almost ready that she realised that she was wearing the wedding-gown that she had worn yesterday, and the tiara on her head, but without the wedding veil.

She looked at Mithra questioningly and the maid said:

"The Prince said, Your Royal Highness, that that is how he wishes you to look. I had brought you a different gown, but this is far more lovely."

The wedding-gown was fortunately completely unsoiled and was not even creased, for the simple reason that it was embroidered all over with tiny *diamantés* which had prevented it from being crushed even though Giōna had ridden up the mountain in it.

In the light of the flares and the moon last night she had appeared to be dressed in silver.

But now, as she walked to the cave where Miklōs was waiting for her, the rays of the sun enveloped her with gold and he seemed to be spellbound as he watched her coming towards him.

"You are so lovely," he said, "that I feel you cannot be real, but I know because you are clothed in gold that you are the Goddess of Hope, and that is what you have given me ever since we first met."

Giōna gave a little laugh, remembering how they had talked together in the dark and how acutely aware she had been of him even though she could not see him.

" 'The Invisible One'," she said softly, "is no longer invisible."

He smiled at her, then helped her down the mountain slope to where in the valley below his people were waiting.

The first thing Giōna saw was an open carriage very much the same as the one in which she had driven with King Ferdinand to the House of Parliament.

As if he guessed what she was thinking Miklōs said:

"You are quite right, I stole it! Or should I perhaps say 'borrowed' it for this special occasion?"

She laughed again at Miklōs's humorous description of his daring, and as she stepped into the carriage she found that the hood which was drawn back was piled with wild flowers.

The same flowers encircled the horses' necks and ornamented the box on which the coachman and a footman were seated.

She was surprised there should be only two horses until as they started she realised they were moving slowly so

136

that Miklōs's followers, and there were a large number walking with them should not be left behind.

Some, it was true, were riding the kind of sturdy little pony on which she had ridden up the mountain, and there were outriders in the shape of four men on each side of the carriage who were dressed as Miklōs had been when she first saw him in the uniform of a Slavonian soldier without any badges of rank or insignia.

She knew when she heard him speaking to them tha. they were his special friends.

It was so early in the morning that the sun was not yet hot, and there was a faint breeze blowing down the valley which made the air fresh and it seemed, Giōna thought, as if they were drinking champagne.

Certainly all those who were travelling with them were in high spirits, and as they walked along keeping pace with the horses they sang songs that were, she was sure, part of Slavonian folklore and known to them since they were children.

It was not a long time before they were joined by people running from the fields, the cottages and the banks of the river.

The women shouted greetings to Miklōs, then joined the crowd walking along behind them.

As they drew nearer and nearer to the City the crowd grew in numbers until the whole countryside seemed to be peopled with those who followed Miklōs.

It was only as they drew nearer the City and could see clearly its roofs and spires that Giōna began to feel afraid.

She imagined that by now King Ferdinand would have had time to rally his troops, and if he intended to fight they would be manning the walls of the City and crouching on the tops of the houses ready with guns and canons to shoot at Miklōs and his followers.

Now feeling really frightened she slipped her hand into

his, and as his fingers closed over hers she felt the strength and comfort of them and knew he was not in the least afraid, but confident that everything would go as he expected.

If she had wanted to talk to him it would have been impossible because of the voices around them singing the songs of Slavonia or cheering, as if only by making a noise could they express their happiness.

Now they were drawing near to the massive gateway into the City, and Giōna looked with frightened eyes expecting to see soldiers posted on it, with perhaps more waiting just inside with their guns at the ready.

She could see people in the distance, but was not certain if they were soldiers or not.

Then as they were almost within the gateway the horses came to a standstill, and she looked at Miklōs, anxiously wondering what was happening.

He drew her to her feet and as he did so riding out from the City came Captain Darius on a black charger.

He galloped up to the side of the carriage and saluted Miklōs before he said:

"Welcome! And that is the right word!"

The Prince drew in his breath and Captain Darius continued:

"King Ferdinand and the majority of his entourage have already fled from the City."

"Where have they gone?"

"Ostensibly to Serbia," Captain Darius replied, "but I think the train will carry them on to Vienna, and we shall not be troubled with them again."

Miklōs seemed for the moment to be still, almost as if he could hardly credit such a thing was true.

But because she had been so frightened and it was such a relief to know the King had actually gone, not only for Miklōs's sake but for her own Giōna gave a cry of sheer happiness.

Then she flung herself against the Prince.

"We have won .. we have won! Oh, Miklōs .. we have .. won! He has .. gone and we need .. no longer be .. afraid."

His arms went round her and as she looked up at him, her eyes shining, the words tumbling out in her excitement, he bent his head and his lips were on hers.

For a second she could hardly believe it was happening.

Then as he kissed her she knew this was what she had been longing for, this was what she had wanted, although she had not been aware of it.

He held her closer still and she felt as if a shaft of sunlight, almost like a streak of lightning, ran through her whole body.

Then she was free and was aware that all around them the people who had been watching were cheering wildly, waving their hats, their handkerchiefs, their caps in the sheer delight of what they had learnt.

The news that Captain Darius had reported was now being passed on to those behind them and the cheers came echoing back to them like waves rippling on a beach.

For a moment, still holding onto Miklōs, Giōna could think of nothing but the wonder of his kiss.

Then she heard him say, speaking calmly in spite of his elation:

"What else have you arranged, Otho?"

"The Archbishop is waiting for you in the Cathedral," Captain Darius replied, "and your joyful subjects are gathered in the Square."

Miklōs smiled.

"Thank you, Otho," he said, "I knew I could rely on you."

"This is the happiest day of my life!" Captain Darius exclaimed.

He saluted, turned his horse and rode away in front of them.

Miklōs drew Giōna down on the seat beside him, and she held onto his hand saying:

"It is true .. really true .. the King has .. gone?"

"He has gone," Miklōs answered, "and he will trouble neither of us again! And now, my beautiful wife, we are to be crowned. After that we have before us the task of bringing this country back to the happiness it knew when my father ruled it."

"I am sure you can do that," Giōna murmured.

"Only with your help," Miklōs said softly.

For a moment their eyes met, and because of the expression in his she felt as if he was kissing her again.

Then as she looked away from him shyly, she was aware of how many people were watching and cheering as they drove into the City and told herself that, whatever she felt about Miklōs, she must remember her duty to them.

When they reached the Square it was so packed with people that it was almost impossible for the horses to move through it.

By now the carriage in which they were driving was almost filled with flowers.

As if by magic every child on either side of the road was holding a flower in its hand and the mothers too had brought little bunches of wild flowers which they threw into the carriage or dropped them over the side as it passed them.

By the time they reached the Cathedral on the other side of the Square and adjacent to the House of Parliament, Giōna thought if there were many more flowers she and Miklōs would be covered by them.

Captain Darius was standing on the Cathedral steps and with him a number of the Clergy.

Behind them were men and women smartly dressed who Giōna guessed must be the Members of Parliament and their wives, and perhaps members of the nobility whom she had not met before.

It was obvious that they were all Slavonian and all rapturously glad to see Miklōs.

They bowed and curtsied to him as the Clergy led the way and they processed up the aisle of the Cathedral, which appeared to be completely packed with people.

At the top of the altar steps stood the Archbishop, who Giōna guessed must have been in retirement until now, waiting for them in the full regalia of the Greek Orthodox Church.

The Chancel was ablaze with candles, but because the seven silver lamps were missing, she guessed that during King Ferdinand's reign, the Services in the Cathedral had been Lutheran.

It was impossible to ask any questions as Miklōs led her in front of the Archbishop and the Coronation began.

Giōna was afraid she would inevitably make mistakes, but one of the Clergy stood beside her to tell her what to do, and after Miklōs had been crowned she knelt before him and he crowned her.

Then as he raised her to her feet and they faced the vast congregation, there was a great shout of welcome from everyone present. It sounded so sincere and so happy that Giōna felt the tears come into her eyes.

There were prayers and the National Anthem was sung. Then still wearing their Royal crowns they moved down the aisle and out onto the steps of the Cathedral to where the people were waiting outside to see them.

If King Miklōs had wanted to speak it would have been impossible, for the cheering and excitement rang out deafeningly and had hardly abated when they turned away to leave their crowns in the Cathedral before they drove away to the Palace.

Somebody took Giōna's crown from her and placed on her head the tiara she had worn when she arrived, and for Miklōs there was a plumed hat which made him look extremely handsome.

At the same time, Giōna thought, there was a new authority about him that had not been there before.

There was a different carriage waiting for them from the one that had brought them from the valley. This was drawn by six white horses with postillions, and it was carved and gilded in a manner which made Giōna aware it was a carriage used only on Royal occasions.

They drove slowly so that everybody on either side of the road could see them and, what was more, there were no soldiers lining the route.

The people ran beside the carriage cheering and throwing flowers into it, and their happiness was so infectious that Giōna felt as if she wanted to cheer too.

"They love you, Miklōs, they love you!" she said when she could make herself heard.

"And they love you too!" he replied. "Do you see how many children have been carrying a rose? You captured their hearts when you accepted the rose from the little boy outside the House of Parliament, then carried him back to his mother."

"You heard about that?"

"A great many people told me," he replied, "but it was Otho Darius who told me about it first."

"I had a feeling, and I was right, that he was your man," Giōna said.

Miklōs laughed.

"He is much more than that! He played an extremely difficult and dangerous part by pretending to be in the King's service while he was actually in mine."

"He is very brave."

"Very!" Miklōs agreed. "In fact, he is my cousin and owns a great deal of land on the Eastern side of the country, but he is not going to be able to enjoy it for a long time."

"Why not?"

"Because I need him here," Miklōs said. "Young though he is, I intend to put him in charge of the Army, and I also need him to help me with many reforms that must be made here in Dūric if the people are to be happy and as well looked after as they should be."

"They need Schools and, I am sure, Hospitals."

"That is going to be one of your jobs."

"Oh, no!" Giōna exclaimed. "Supposing I make a mess of it?"

"I will look after you," Miklōs promised. "You may be certain of that."

There was a look in his eyes that made her once again feel shy.

There was no chance of saying any more for by now they had reached the Palace where again Captain Darius was waiting for them with a large number of Slavonian dignitaries who, she learnt later, had refused to work under King Ferdinand, but were now willing and eager to do anything that was required of them.

They had a great deal to say during luncheon, which was a delicious but short meal, and the only speech was made by the new King.

He thanked them for their loyalty and told them that he intended tomorrow to start immediately on reforms which he believed were long overdue.

It was late in the afternoon when finally Giōna was able to go upstairs to take off her tiara which by now, even though it was light, was beginning to make her head ache.

"Go and rest," Miklōs said to her. "Mithra is waiting for you and will tell you what I have planned for the evening."

Giōna wanted to protest and say that she would rather be with him alone, but she thought he might refuse her request and that would be embarrassing.

She felt for the moment exhausted at meeting so many

people, however kind and congratulatory they had been.

When she reached the top of the Grand Staircase it was a relief to see Mithra waiting for her.

The woman did not curtsy but went down on her knees and kissed her hand saying:

"I pledge myself, Your Majesty, to serve you now and for ever not only with loyalty, but with love."

Giōna made a sound that was almost a sob as she said: "Thank you, Mithra. I am afraid I am very tired."

"I know, Your Majesty, and I have everything ready. Come!"

She guided Giōna along the passage and in the direction of the room she had had before, but into another which, when she realised it, Giōna knew must have been shut up during King Ferdinand's occupation of the Palace.

There were maids still removing the Holland covers from the furniture and brushing and dusting the rooms through which they passed.

When she finally came to her own bedroom she knew why they had not been used.

They were all exquisitely beautiful in a manner which would certainly not have appealed to the Germanic tastes of King Ferdinand.

The ceilings were painted with goddesses and cupids, the furniture was antique French, and the pictures were mostly by famous French artists.

The Aubusson carpets and the pale damask hangings were patterned in delicate colours.

In Giōna's room the bed was carved with cupids, doves and flowers all heavily gilded, and the curtains were of blue silk, the colour of the sky.

In fact, everywhere she looked there were emblems of love.

She knew without being told it was a room that Miklōs would remember as a boy and had been his mother's.

Then because she was very tired she allowed Mithra to

undress her and put on one of the attractive nightgowns which her mother had bought for her in Bond Street.

She slipped into bed and almost as soon as her head touched the pillow she was asleep.

She seemed to have slept for a very long time before Mithra awoke her, and she realised the sun was setting and it must be growing late in the evening.

"Your bath is ready, Your Majesty," Mithra said, "and I have a message from His Majesty."

Giōna was suddenly alert.

"What is it?"

"His Majesty has arranged for you to dine together in the *Boudoir* this evening."

"Alone?"

"Alone, Your Majesty."

Giōna jumped out of bed no longer tired but filled with excitement that was different from anything she had known before.

She had been so afraid that because it was the first evening of Miklōs's reign they would have to have a large dinner-party, and there would be no chance of talking to him or even of sitting beside him.

Now she would be able to say to him all the things that seemed to have crowded into her mind, and she could hardly wait to enjoy the flower-scented bath which Mithra had ready for her.

When she had dried herself she found Mithra waiting with, not as she expected, one of her elaborate evening-gowns but a negligée and a nightgown that matched it.

"Can I really wear that?" Giōna asked.

"But of course, Your Majesty! Then you can relax and there will be no one to see you except His Majesty."

This however made Giōna feel rather shy as she left her bedroom and went into the *Boudoir* where she had been told the King was waiting for her.

He rose from his chair as she came in, and she saw

145

that the room was as beautiful as her bedroom and had been decorated with white flowers whose fragrance scented the air.

But it was impossible to look at anything except the man who was her husband, and whom she had kissed from sheer excitement when she learned that he had won the battle against his adversary and that no one had been killed or injured.

"You are rested?" Miklōs asked in his deep voice.

"I am afraid I was very tired."

"You had every reason to be," he answered. "Come and sit down and let me give you a glass of champagne."

He put a glass into her hand and as she sipped it he said:

"I thought, as we have been surrounded by people all day, tonight we would be alone, really alone. Then we can talk and we are going to wait on ourselves, or rather, I am going to wait on you. In that way, my lovely one, we shall not be disturbed."

It was something Giōna had not expected and her eyes lit up as she said:

"That will be very .. exciting!"

"That is what I hoped you would think," Miklōs said, "and let me start by telling you that you look even more beautiful at this moment than you did today in the Cathedral, where, as I crowned you, I thought that no Slavonian Queen had ever been lovelier."

"I felt I was crowned with love," Giōna said, thinking of the crowds inside and outside the Cathedral who were so thrilled by what had happened.

"You must have read my thoughts," Miklōs said in a deep voice, "and I am sure no Queen has ever been more worthy of her throne than you."

"You are making me feel very shy and embarrassed," Giōna said. "I know how ignorant I am, but I am relying on you to .. teach me what I .. should do."

"I have every intention of doing that," Miklōs said, "and there are in fact many things I want to teach you."

He spoke in his deep voice in a manner which made Giōna drop her eyes.

After a moment's hesitation he rose and fetched the dishes from a side-table on which they were being kept warm by little candles burning beneath the silver dishes themselves.

Afterwards Giōna found it impossible to remember what she did eat, except that it was delicious, because she was acutely conscious of Miklōs sitting opposite her.

The candlelight was shining on his handsome face and seemed to bring a strange gleam to his eyes when he looked into hers.

When their dinner was finished, Miklōs rang the bell and immediately servants appeared to carry away the table and everything else in the passing of seconds.

Then as they shut the door behind them he sat down beside Giōna on the low sofa and said:

"Now we can talk to each other!"

"That is what I have been wanting to do," Giōna said with a smile, "but there were far too many other people who wanted to tell you what they were thinking and feeling."

"How could I have hoped that everything would go so smoothly," Miklōs said, "and exactly as I had planned?"

"You really believed that King Ferdinand would run away?" Giōna asked.

"I hoped and prayed that he would do so once the Army had deserted," Miklōs replied. "But as you can imagine, it was a great relief to know that there need be no fighting in which a number of our people might be killed. They have suffered enough already."

"I am sure they will soon forget it and be happy now that you are on the throne," Giōna said.

"There is a great deal to do," Miklōs answered, "but

fortunately I have people like Otho Darius, who have been loyal to me all through the years in exile and who will now reap their reward."

He paused before he went on:

"What is more important now, Giōna, is for us to talk about ourselves."

Then as Giōna gave a sigh of relief because she was fascinated and at the same time afraid of what he might say, she rose to her feet and walked across the *Boudoir* to the window.

She pulled back the damask curtain to look out at the moonlight.

Below her she could see the gardens of the Palace and beyond them the iron railings which separated the Palace from the City.

In every street and every house, it seemed to her, the lights were burning, and faintly as if from a long way off she could hear music. She was sure the people were dancing and celebrating excitedly their new King, a new reign, and a new era of happiness.

Lost in thought she started a little as she realised that Miklōs had followed her and was standing beside her.

"What are you thinking now?"

"I was thinking how happy they are."

"And what about us, Giōna?"

"How could you be anything but happy now that you are the King?"

"And you?"

"You know how happy I am now that I need .. no longer be .. afraid."

He knew she was thinking of King Ferdinand and he said very quietly:

"Forget him, he belongs to the past. Think of me, because I am the future."

"I am thinking of .. you."

"In what way?"

"That you are very .. wonderful .. very brave and I am so glad .. so very .. very glad that the Fairy Story has come true."

"Are you sure about that?"

"Of course I am sure."

"And you know how Fairy Stories end?"

Her eyes flickered and she looked away from him as he said softly:

"'And they lived happily ever after'. Is that what we are going to do, Giōna?"

She found it impossible to answer, but she felt his arms go round her very gently as if he had no wish to frighten her.

Then as her face was still turned away from him he touched her chin with his fingers and turned it up to his.

"You are so absurdly beautiful," he said, "and at the same time so intelligent! Who else would have behaved as you did during what would have been a terrifying ordeal for a woman twice your age?"

Giōna felt herself quiver because he was touching her and because his arms were around her.

There were so many things she wanted to say to him, but she felt as if her voice had died in her throat and it was impossible to find words to say what was in her heart.

"Today," Miklōs said, still in that quiet voice, "you kissed me because you were so glad that we were no longer in danger. I would like to think that you kissed me for another reason."

He felt her tremble, but she did not speak and after a moment he asked:

"Because you love me?"

She wanted to hide her face against him, but he prevented her from doing so. Instead he said:

"I will say it first – I love you, my darling! And the only way I can express my love is by kissing you."

As he spoke his lips came down on hers, and without thinking, without really meaning to, she pressed herself closer to him and felt his arms tighten.

Then his lips which were at first very tender and gentle as if she was something infinitely precious and he was afraid of frightening her, became more intense, more demanding.

Now the sunlight was streaking through her body, so vividly, so acutely, that it was almost a pain as well as an indescribable pleasure.

He kissed her until she felt the whole world was whirling around them and they were being carried up into the sky, until at last he raised his head to say in a voice that was curiously unsteady:

"I love you, my beautiful wife! Now tell me what you feel about me."

"I .. love .. you."

It was difficult to say the words and they were only a whisper, but she saw his eyes light up as if they were on fire.

Then he was kissing her again, kissing her demandingly, fiercely, as if he was afraid of losing her.

It was so perfect and so wonderful that she thought she must be dreaming and it could not in fact, be true.

How could she possibly in this Palace of all places, feel so happy?

"I .. I love you .. I love .. you!" she cried when Miklōs released her.

He drew in his breath before he said:

"I feel as though I have loved you for a million years, and you will never know how frightened I was that you would not love me."

"When did you first love me?" she asked as she pressed herself close against him.

"I suppose really I fell in love with you when Otho told me about you and how young and innocent you were,

150

and at the same time so intelligent. I was also captivated by the pictures of you in the newspapers, although they were very bad sketches, my darling, and not half as beautiful as you are in reality!"

"So you .. thought of me before we met in the .. railway carriage?"

"It was because I thought about you," Miklōs said, "that when I heard what my people intended, I knew I could not let them destroy you. It was a crazy idea which I would never have sanctioned if I had had the slightest hint that was what they planned."

"So you saved me, as I saved you."

"I knew when I talked to you in the train," he said, "that you were everything that a Queen should be, and I was almost tempted to give up fighting for my rightful place because I thought that if you ruled over my people they would be safe without me."

"How could you have thought of anything so .. terrifying as to .. leave me with .. him?"

Miklōs drew in his breath.

"I had no idea that he would treat you with anything but respect and propriety, even though I knew how bestial he was in his private life."

He felt Giōna give a shudder of horror and he said:

"Forget him! The only thing we have to think about at this moment, my darling, is ourselves, our happiness and our love!"

He accentuated the last word and Giōna looked up at him as she said:

"I do love you .. I love you as I always .. wanted to love the man to whom I was married .. but thought because I am Royal it would be .. impossible. Mama said that to marry without love was the penalty we paid for our position, yet I prayed I would be the .. exception."

"Your prayers have been answered," Miklōs said, "for

I shall love, adore and worship you for the rest of our lives. Will that be enough?"

"Only if we .. live a million years together," Giōna said passionately. "Oh, Miklōs .. I am so .. happy!"

"That is what I want you to feel, and I adore you, my sweet little Queen."

He held her close to him and she thought that he was going to kiss her again. But instead he said in a very serious tone:

"I thought perhaps after I had talked to you and told you how much I loved you, you should rest, and I should leave you alone. Is that what you want?"

Giōna hid her face against his shoulder as she said in a voice he could hardly hear:

"I .. I want to be .. with you."

"You are sure of that? I told you last night, and it seems a long time ago, that perhaps we should first get to know each other as friends. I think now, my precious one, we have passed the stage of friendship, or am I mistaken?"

"I .. I want to be your .. friend .. I want to do things with you," Giōna said, "and I .. also want you to .. love me .. really love me."

She knew Miklōs's heart was beating feverishly as hers was as she went on:

"You will think I am .. very ignorant, but Mama did not tell me .. exactly what .. happens when a man and a woman .. make love to each .. other .. and although it must be .. horrible and obscene with somebody one does not .. love .. with you I know it will be .. different."

"Oh, my darling heart, are you sure of that?" Miklōs asked. "You are so very young and I am desperately afraid of frightening or shocking you."

Giōna shook her head.

"I do not .. think you could do that and .. when you kiss me .. I feel as if your .. kisses carry me into the sky

152

and are .. part of the sunshine .. the stars and everything that is .. beautiful .. and I am sure your love-making will be very much the same."

Miklōs shut his eyes for a moment as if he could hardly believe what he was hearing.

Then very gently he picked Giōna up in his arms and carried her through the communicating door into her bedroom.

There were only two candles to light the room burning beside the beautiful gold bed. He put her on her feet, very gently pulled off her negligée and then picked her up again and laid her down against the soft pillows.

Then as she looked up at him wide-eyed, her mystical eyes seeming to fill the Grecian oval of her face, he said:

"I worship you! There is no other word to describe what I feel. It is true, Giōna, there have been many women in my life while I have been waiting for you, but I have never felt about any of them as I feel now about you."

Giōna held onto him almost as if she was afraid he might leave her and begged:

"Tell me .. what you .. do feel."

"I want to look after you and protect you," Miklōs said, "not only from anything that might hurt or frighten you, but also a little from myself. Love is not quiet and gentle here, like it is in England, but a force strong, irresistible, and at times uncontrollable! I know that what I feel for you is greater than myself, greater than both of us. It comes from a power that is omnipotent, and we have no defence against it."

She was looking at him wide-eyed as he looked down at her and said:

"If you want me to wait a little longer before I show you how much I love you, before I make you completely and absolutely mine, I will, because I have laid my heart and my life at your feet, obey you. But it will be very difficult not to let you realise how deep, strong and passionate my love for you already is."

As he finished speaking he raised himself up a little and Giōna felt as if he was already leaving her, already going away, and she would be alone.

She lifted up her arms and put them around his neck.

"It is not a question of how long we have known each other, Miklōs," she said, "it is that at the very moment you came near me in the dark, I could feel your vibrations reaching out towards me, as mine reached out to you. I knew then in a strange way not only that I could trust you, but somehow I .. belonged to you, as I belong to you now. I love you .. I love you! Please stay .. with me and .. tell me of your .. love."

As she finished speaking something seemed to break in Miklōs.

He bent forward to take her fiercely into his arms and crush her against him.

Then he was kissing her with wild, passionate, demanding kisses that seemed to draw not only her heart from her body but also her soul, her very life and make it his.

And yet she was not afraid.

She could feel the fire burning in him and something leapt within her to meet it, and the flames carried them wildly up into the sky.

It was impossible to think, but only to feel and to love.

. . . . . . .

A long time later when the candles had burnt low Miklōs said in a voice deep with emotion:

"My precious, my darling, my adorable little wife, do you still love me?"

Giōna laughed and it was a very happy sound.

"How can you ask such a foolish question? Oh, Miklōs,

154

I had no idea that . . love was so wonderful . . so perfect."

He held her a little closer to him before she went on:

"I . . I did not . . disappoint you . . or do anything that was wrong?"

"How could you think of anything so ridiculous, my lovely one?" he said. "I have never, and this is true, been so happy, and like you I never knew that love could be so perfect, so utterly and completely supreme."

Giōna gave a little sigh.

"Now I understand all the things I have read about love, the music that expresses it, the pictures that try to depict it on canvas."

She threw back her head to look up at her husband as she said:

"If you should . . ever stop . . loving me . . I know I would . . no longer want to . . live."

"There is no fear of that," Miklōs replied. "I think, my darling one, we were made for each other from the beginning of time, and fate has been drawing us together over the centuries until at last, after hundreds of lives in which we have striven to do what was right, we are now in a position in which we have the power to help other people and bring to this country a happiness which will influence and inspire everyone who lives here."

He spoke very solemnly and Giōna said:

"You . . really believe . . that?"

"I believe that is what we can achieve together. Our love will create love in other people, especially those who admire and serve us."

Giōna gave a little cry.

"Oh, Miklōs, that is a beautiful idea! All I want is to love you and go on loving you and as you love me . . and it will not be very difficult."

He smiled before he said:

"Because we are human there will be difficulties. But, darling, I think that just as we have surmounted a great many obstacles already, we shall be able to surmount any more that stand in our way."

"That is what we must do."

Then she said in a different tone of voice:

"You promised that tonight we should think of nobody but ourselves, and I want to be selfish and just say 'I love you!' Please, Miklōs, love me!"

"That is a very easy thing to do," he said, "because I love you so much already that you fill my whole world. In fact at the moment I cannot believe there is a Kingdom waiting for me to rule it."

He looked down at her in the dying light as he said:

"All I want to do, my darling one, is to make love to you until you love me a thousand times more than you do already and very nearly as much as I love you."

"That is . . impossible," Giōna smiled.

"No, it is what is going to happen, and I will prove it very easily."

As Miklōs spoke he kissed first her little winged eyebrows, then her eyes and her straight little Grecian nose. Then, although her lips were parted waiting for his, he bent lower still and kissed the softness of her neck.

It gave her a strange feeling she had not known before, and she stirred a little beneath him until as if he could not help himself his lips found hers.

Then as he kissed her with a passion that was even more intense than when he had kissed her before, she felt his heart beating against hers.

She knew he was right when he had said that love was irresistible and uncontrollable.

She could feel the fire within her responding to the fire in him.

As they burned together in the flames of love, Giōna knew this was the love they had sought through Eternity and would continue on to Eternity, world without end.

# THE DEVIL DEFEATED

The Earl laughed and it was a very tender sound. Then he said:

"Oh, my darling, only you could give an answer like that, which is so true, but at the same time is not really what I wanted to hear."

At the endearment Dorina's eyes widened in surprise and he said:

"Surely you realise now that what I am trying to say in a roundabout way is that I love you."

"You .. love .. me?"

The words were only a murmur beneath her breath, but her face was suddenly radiant with an almost strange unearthly happiness.